Chip Hilton Sports Series

#18

Triple-Threat Trouble

Coach Clair Bee

Foreword by Jack McCallum

Updated by Randall and Cynthia Bee Farley

BROADMAN
& HOLMAN
PUBLISHERS

Nashville, Tennessee

Printed in the United States of America

0-8054-2097-5

Published by Broadman & Holman Publishers,
Nashville, Tennessee

Subject Heading: FOOTBALL—FICTION / YOUTH
Library of Congress Card Catalog Number: 00-068882

Library of Congress Cataloging-in-Publication Data

Bee, Clair.
Triple-threat trouble / Clair Bee ; updated by Randall and Cynthia Bee Farley ; foreword by Jack McCallum.
p. cm. — (Chip Hilton sports series ; #18)
Summary: Chip Hilton proves his worth to the State University football team off the field, as well as on, when he helps a talented high school player make a big decision and shows two new team members the importance of working together.
ISBN 0-8054-2097-5 (pb)
[1. Football—Fiction. 2. Teamwork (Sports)—Fiction.]
I. Farley, Randall K., 1952– . II. Farley, Cynthia Bee, 1952– .
III. Title.

PZ7.B38196 Tr 2001
[Fic]—dc21 00-068882

1 2 3 4 5 6 7 8 9 10 05 04 03 02 01

The Chip Hilton Sports Series

Touchdown Pass
Championship Ball
Strike Three!
Clutch Hitter!
A Pass and a Prayer
Hoop Crazy
Pitchers' Duel
Dugout Jinx
Freshman Quarterback
Backboard Fever
Fence Busters
Ten Seconds to Play!
Fourth Down Showdown
Tournament Crisis
Hardcourt Upset
Pay-Off Pitch
No-Hitter
Triple-Threat Trouble
Backcourt Ace
Buzzer Basket
Comeback Cagers
Home Run Feud
Hungry Hurler
Fiery Fullback

For more information on
Coach Clair Bee and **Chip Hilton**
please visit us at
www.chiphilton.com

Lou Little

Great coach, friend, gentleman,
and sportsman.

COACH CLAIR BEE, 1960

John Moffet and Karen Plunkett-Powell

and to all the wonderful members
of the South Jersey Series Collectors

With gratitude,
RANDY AND CINDY, 2001

Contents

Foreword

IT'S SOMETIMES difficult to figure out why we became who we became. Was it an influential teacher who steered you toward biology? A beloved grandparent who turned you into a machinist? A motorcycle accident that forced you into accounting?

All I know is that in my case the Chip Hilton books had something—no, a lot—to do with my becoming a sports journalist. At the very least, the books got me to sit down and read when others of my generation were watching television or otherwise goofing off; at most, they taught me many of life's lessons, about sports and sportsmanship, about coaches and coaching, about winning and losing.

Also, the books helped me, quite literally, get the job I have now. Over two decades ago, when I was a sportswriter at a small newspaper in Pennsylvania, I interviewed Clair Bee and wrote a piece about him and the Hilton books. For some strange reason, even before I met Clair, I knew I could make the story memorable, knew that meeting a legend like Clair and plumbing his mind for memories were going to be magic. They were. I sold the story to *Sports Illustrated,* and, partly because of it, I was later hired there full time.

To my surprise, and especially to the surprise of the editors at *SI,* the story produced a torrent of letters, hundreds of them, all written by closet Clair and Chip fans who, like me, had grown up on the books and never been able to forget them. Since the piece about Clair appeared in 1979, I've written hundreds of other articles, many of them cover stories about famous athletes like Michael Jordan, Magic Johnson, and Larry Bird; yet I'm still known, by and large, as the "guy who wrote the Chip Hilton story." I would safely say that still, two decades later, six months do not go by that I don't receive some kind of question about Clair and Chip.

One of the many fortunate things that happened to me as a result of that story was meeting Clair's daughter, Cindy Farley, and her husband, Randy, as well as others who could recite the starting lineups of Coach Rockwell's Valley Falls teams.

I am proud to have played a small part in the revival of Chip and the restoration of interest in Clair (not that real basketball people ever forget him). It's hard to put a finger on what exactly endures from the books, but it occurs to me that what Clair succeeded in doing was to create a universe of which we would all like to be a part.

As I leafed through one of the books recently, a memory came back to me from my days as a twelve-year-old Pop Warner football player in Mays Landing, New Jersey. A friend who shared my interest in the books had just thrown an opposing quarterback for a loss in a key game. As we walked back to the huddle, he put his arm on my shoulder pads and, conjuring up a Hilton gang character, whispered, "Another jarring tackle by Biggie Cohen." No matter how old you get, you never forget something like that. Thank you, Clair Bee.

JACK McCALLUM
Senior Writer, *Sports Illustrated*

CHAPTER 1

Triple-Threat Triplets

THE CHAUFFEUR muttered something unintelligible to the teenager sitting beside him in the front seat and irritably slowed the long, black airport limo to a stop. A young man, about nineteen years old, was standing in the middle of the road holding up a hand to stop the car.

He was wearing a blue sweatshirt decorated with a big red *S* and carrying an official-looking clipboard under his arm. Behind him, the road was blocked by a white gate attached to a rustic arch on which CAMP SUNDOWN was painted in bright red and blue letters.

"Excuse me," he said, smiling apologetically, "I'm one of the State University managers. I have to stop *everyone*."

"Mr. E. Merton Blaine's party," the chauffeur said haughtily, gesturing toward the distinguished looking man who sat directly behind him.

The young man checked the list he was carrying and shook his head. "Mr. Blaine's name isn't here," he said, peering curiously at the blond teenager sitting in the front passenger seat.

A man sitting in the back seat quickly leaned forward. "It's OK. I'm Coach Bill Carpenter," he said, "from University High School."

He held out a sheet of paper. "This might help. It's a letter from Coach Ralston—"

The manager glanced at the letter and smiled. "That's the ticket. No doubt about that," he said. "He's the boss around here." He nodded toward the boy in the front seat. "Wow! *You* look like—"

"We know, we know. He looks like that Chip Hilton fellow," Blaine interrupted abruptly, removing an expensive cigar from his mouth. "Well, you're right. He looks like Hilton, walks like Hilton, talks like Hilton, and plays football like Hilton. Further, he thinks like Hilton when he's playing quarterback and running the team. But he's my nephew, Coleman Merton Miller, *not* this Hilton individual."

"Uncle Merton," the teenage boy smiled and interjected, "you know everybody calls me 'Skip.' You gave me that nickname years ago."

"He's a triple-threat star too," Carpenter added. "Skip made all-state the last two years."

The manager's interest increased. "He's going out for the freshman team, isn't he?"

Coach Carpenter laughed. "Freshman team? Not yet! He's got another year at University High School, thank goodness. Skip's playing means another state championship for us."

Mr. Blaine tossed his hand impatiently in the driver's direction. "*Freshman team?*" he retorted. "My nephew has already been contacted by some very fine football schools who have assured him of a varsity starting spot. He's *not* wasting a valuable season playing with a bunch of freshmen at State University."

"Well, he sure looks like Hilton to me," the manager said. "Same blond hair and gray eyes. He looks enough like Chip to be a younger brother."

"Nearly as big as Hilton, too," Carpenter said proudly. "Six-two, 185—"

As the car moved on, Blaine snorted and chucked his cigar out the window. "How about that!" he said in disgust. "They're checking every car! Just for a practice session. You'd think we were trying to get in to see the president of the United States."

"Coach Ralston takes his football pretty seriously," Carpenter said.

"Small-time stuff," Blaine said shortly. "Stew Peterson *invites* the public in to see his practices. The more the merrier."

"Coach Peterson has developed a big-time program all right," Carpenter said in admiration.

"Stew Peterson and Brand University are *both* big time," Blaine said proudly. "Wait until Skip sees Brand's football program. Makes this place look like a picnic area . . . and the campus! It's one of the prettiest in the country."

Skip had been listening quietly. Now he joined in the conversation. "Brand's a nice place, but it's a long way from home, Uncle Merton," he ventured.

"Not by plane," Blaine said quickly. "That's the way you would be traveling. You know how often I make the trip in my plane. Averages about four or five times a month. Another passenger back and forth wouldn't mean a thing. In fact, it would be company for Riggs. He's crazy about football."

Blaine turned to Carpenter. "Riggs is my personal pilot. You've met him."

"But I wouldn't know anyone out there," Skip persisted.

"Nonsense!" Blaine replied impatiently. "The whole campus would know you in a week. As far as that's concerned," he continued thoughtfully, "your father could move the whole family out there. Fixing him up with a good job in the main plant would be easy."

Skip stared unfocused out the window as Uncle Merton continued.

"Listen, State's freshman pilot program is good in theory, but you don't need all that guidance from a school. I can take care of that when you're at Brand. Your grades are good, and you're ready to play Division 1 football at the varsity level without waiting a year."

"It's a good thing Coach Ralston can't hear you talking to Skip," Bill Carpenter said, laughing nervously. "He's hoping your nephew will attend State."

Skip turned away from the window and looked back at his coach. "I can't make up my mind what to do."

Before Bill Carpenter could reply, E. Merton Blaine announced, "There's plenty of time for that, and besides, I'll help you. Don't worry about it."

He turned to Carpenter. "Getting back to Ralston, he's a rookie compared to Peterson. It's all a matter of record. Stew Peterson makes Curly Ralston's program look small-time."

"Maybe so," Carpenter said in an accommodating tone of voice, "but he's the biggest thing that's happened to State football in a long time. Last year was only his second, but he won the conference title. He might do it again this year too."

"You mean *Chip Hilton* might do it," Skip said pointedly.

"I thought it took eleven men to make a team," Blaine said, winking significantly at Carpenter.

"To make a team, yes," Skip retorted. "But it takes a guy like Hilton to make a team *great.* I saw every game State played last year—"

"And almost every practice session!" Carpenter interrupted. "I don't know what you would have done if we hadn't played our games on Fridays."

"Granted, Hilton was a sensation as a sophomore," Blaine said lightly, "but it doesn't mean he can repeat."

"He can repeat," Skip said stubbornly. "Why shouldn't he? He was on everybody's all-America team—"

"Hilton doesn't know it," Carpenter said, "but he made you the best high school quarterback in the country."

"But Skip was all-state the year before," Blaine pointed out.

"Sure," Carpenter agreed, "but he picked up a lot of all-around finesse from Hilton. Getting back to this year, though, you might be right about Hilton and State. Ralston lost a lot of players; more than a third of the squad graduated."

"That proves my point," Blaine proclaimed. "Peterson has his players at Brand for four years. This pilot program at State gives Ralston only three years to work with his players."

"It doesn't mean a thing," Skip said knowingly, grinning back at the two men. "Chip Hilton is still around."

The car moved along the tree-lined road, past a number of cabins, and out into a wide, cleared field. On one side of the field were several large one-story buildings and, below these, a little river with a slow-moving current. On the other side of the field were several tennis and basketball courts. In the center of the open area was a football field enclosed by temporary stands on each side.

"I thought we'd be early," Blaine said in surprise, staring at the nearly filled bleachers.

"It's hard to beat the State fans," Carpenter grinned. "Most of them practically live down here during training camp. State used to hold all their practices at the university, but they came down here a year ago when the State fields were being worked on. Ralston likes practicing down here without any distractions."

Although it was only early August and the sun was warm and bright, there was a hint of football weather in the faint, cool breeze that drifted gently off the nearby mountain ridge. Blaine and his two companions walked around the field and climbed to the top row of the bleachers. They had an unobstructed view of the players and soon were pointing them out to one another.

"There's Chip Hilton!" Skip said excitedly. "On the other side of the field. That's him punting now. Man, what a boot!"

"The other kicker is Fireball Finley, the fullback," Carpenter added. "He's almost as good as Hilton."

"He might kick as far," Skip protested, "but he doesn't boot 'em as high. And he hasn't got the same control. Chip can angle 'em out of bounds inside the ten-yard line any time. I've seen him do it more than once."

"Seems to me there's several good kickers out there," Blaine observed. "These two right down in front don't look too bad either."

Carpenter studied the two kickers. "They're new to me," he said, shaking his head. "I've never seen them before. You know them, Skip?"

Skip shook his head. "No, Coach. They must be up from last year's freshman team. Hey, one of those guys kicks lefty! He can boot 'em too."

Over on the other side of the field, Fireball Finley kicked the ball again. The loud plunk of his shoe meeting the pigskin attracted their attention. The ball took off on a long, low trajectory. "Forty-five to fifty yards," Carpenter said, "like a bullet."

Down below, the right-footed kicker took his turn, and they shifted their attention to watch the result. The kick covered about the same distance as Finley's. It was the lefty kicker's turn now, but he paused to watch Hilton on the other side of the field.

The snap shot back to the tall, slender quarterback, and he gave it all he had, his leg following through until his foot ended high above his head. The ball took off and up and out, wobbling and spinning high into the air until it reached its highest point. It seemed to hang there for a second and then darted wickedly downward, gliding and slipping deceptively from side to side. The receiver suddenly turned and ran backward, but he wasn't fast enough. The ball soared far over his head.

"It's way over Speed Morris's head," Skip breathed, his voice filled with awe. "And Morris is *fast!*"

"A mile high too," Carpenter added.

The lefty kicker took his turn. It was a good, solid boot, but it couldn't compare with Hilton's tremendous kick. "I've seen that player somewhere," Carpenter mused, "but I can't place him."

He turned toward two men who were sitting a few feet away. "Do either of you know the names of the two kickers right down in front of us? Where are they from?"

The nearest man grinned and elbowed the man next to him. "We sure do," he said eagerly. "The one kicking with his left foot is my son, Travis Aker, and the other boy is Jack Jacobs." He gestured with his thumb toward his friend. "His son. We're all from Burton. The kids played together in high school. They're halfbacks, and they both run, pass, and kick. Guess you saw for yourself how well they can kick the ball. Travis plays right half and runs and passes to the left. Jack plays left half and runs and passes to the right."

He took a deep breath, and before Carpenter could speak, continued hurriedly, "They're real hard runners too. Our boys even played defensive backs on the frosh squad last season, so they can block and tackle with the best of them. You just wait until you see them fire the ball. And both of them can do something Hilton can't do. They can pass the ball on the dead run and knock your eye out with it every time."

Skip snorted quietly in disgust. "No way," he said, turning away.

Aker glanced sharply at the youngster and went on. "Yes sir, they just about tore every team they met to pieces last year with the freshman team. You see the size of them? They're two of a kind. Both of them are six feet and weigh 190. The newspapers labeled them the touchdown twins. All they need is a little help and a couple of good plays.

"I don't know what kind of a system the coach is going to use this year now that he's got our two boys. Heaven knows we had enough college recruiters parking themselves in our living rooms or ringing our phones off the hook the last couple of years they were in high school." Aker paused for breath and then quickly continued. "If you ask me, Curly Ralston would be a fool *not* to build his offense around our boys."

Fred Jacobs pounced on Ed Aker's last word. "It makes no difference what kind of a system Ralston uses. He's still gonna have a tough time keeping our two kids off the field and out of his starting lineup."

Carpenter leaned close to Blaine, their heads nearly touching. "Coach Ralston's going to have a rough time keeping these two fathers from doing the coaching too," he added softly.

Before Bill Carpenter could thank the two men, Mr. Aker took off again. "Yes, sir," he said loudly, glancing around. "When you put our two kids in the same backfield with Chip Hilton and then add a line in front of them, you'll really have something. Imagine! Three triple-threat players in the *same* backfield!

"Mark my words: As soon as Ralston wakes up and puts Travis and Jack and Chip Hilton together, the sportswriters all over the country will start calling them the triple-threat triplets. Just like years ago when everyone called those Notre Dame greats the Four Horsemen. How about that! The *triple-threat triplets!*"

CHAPTER 2

Fair-Haired Boy

COACH RALSTON'S shrill whistle cut across the field, and his "On the double!" brought Chip, Fireball, Mike Brennan, Speed, and the rest of the squad on the run to surround him in the center of the field. The tall, well-built man waited until the players quieted.

"All right!" he barked. "Get your helmets and hustle down to the north goal. Before we get lined up for our intrasquad scrimmage, we're going to have the 'challenge' break. Coach Nelson and Coach Sullivan are going to split you into groups. Coaches, divide them up! Backs and ends together. Guards, tackles, and centers. Coach Rockwell will be with me. We'll check the winners of the challenge at the other end of the field."

Chip turned and headed for the north goal, and the other backs followed his lead. Speed and Fireball sprinted up beside him with Ace Gibbons trailing on their heels.

Fireball jogged next to Chip. "Remember the first time we raced?" he asked, grinning.

"I knew you'd remind me of that!" Chip said with a sigh. "You beat me."

"It was the first and last time," Fireball said wryly, "*and* I had an assist. A would-be friend of mine bumped into you accidentally *on purpose*. Remember?"

"I remember," Chip said, stopping at the goal line. "So, what about this time?"

Before Fireball could reply, Ace Gibbons chimed in. "What is this?" he interrupted teasingly. "A private race? How about Speed and me?"

Travis Aker and Jack Jacobs were close enough to hear the kidding. They looked at each other and mocked their surprise.

"I thought *everyone* was supposed to run," Aker said pointedly.

"Oh, no," Jacobs said sarcastically. "You heard what Mr. Gibbons said. This is a private race. You know—*returning varsity stars only.*"

"But according to Ralston, *every* position is open."

"*Ralston?*" Aker repeated mockingly. "What's he got to do with it?"

"Why, Travis, you know him," Jacobs said loudly. "He's the coach—"

Ace Gibbons had taken as much as he would stand. He squared his shoulders and moved slowly and purposefully toward the two young, cynical halfbacks. "If you two guys think you're being funny—"

Ace didn't have a chance to finish the sentence. Nik Nelson and Jim Sullivan, the assistant coaches, had reached the goal line. Nelson's "Knock off the silly stuff! Let's go!" broke up the brewing unpleasantness.

"Backs and ends first," he called out. "Move up to the goal line, and keep your helmets on. Use a three-point stance. Take off on the third 'hut!' Guards, centers, and tackles, your challenge is from the fifty."

Chip lined up between Speed and Fireball. Gibbons was beside the big fullback, and the rest of the backs and ends were strung out along the goal line. The coaches had given the squad wind sprints from the first day of camp, but this was the first real challenge.

Chip glanced along the line, trying to figure out his personal competition. Speed, Fireball, Ace, Red Schwartz, Whittemore, and Junior Roberts were old teammates. He knew what they could do. Speed Morris, his friend since elementary school in Valley Falls, and Fireball were extremely fast, evenly matched, and capable of beating him in any race. If he got a bad start, he was in danger of following one or both of them across the opposite goal line.

Ace, Red, Whitty, and Junior Roberts were four of a kind—all slow at the start. But once they got started, all were equipped with plenty of strength, speed, leg drive, and heart to fight to the very end. Chip had thrown passes to Chris "Monty" Montague, and the slender sophomore end had shown enough to convince everyone that he could run. Chip knew nothing about his own understudy, Gary Young, but the fiery sophomore quarterback seemed fast. So far, Aker and Jacobs hadn't really shown much. They spent most of their time bragging about their past accomplishments and ridiculing other players.

"Ready, men? Into your stances. Hut, hut, *hut!*"

Chip took three short digging steps and gradually lengthened his stride. He was concentrating on a straight line to the other end of the field, but he was aware that Speed and Fireball were even with him. He didn't turn his head, but out of the corner of his eye he could see daylight behind the two sprinters, and he knew the three of them were out in front.

They were across the thirty, the forty, the midfield stripe, and Speed and Fireball still kept pace. Now the forty . . . .

Chip heard a roar from the sideline stands then, and his heart jumped as Aker and Jacobs shot slightly ahead ten yards to his left.

He was still a stride behind Aker and Jacobs when he crossed the thirty, and Speed and Fireball were no longer beside him. Then, for the first time, he stepped up the pace, beginning his final push. There wasn't any use worrying about Aker, Jacobs, Speed, Fireball, or anyone else now. It was a matter of going full steam ahead, pumping his arms, lifting his knees high, and putting out his last ounce of strength.

Chip sped across the twenty, the fifteen, the ten, the five, and the goal line and slowed only after he was a few strides beyond the end zone. Then he turned to see how the others had made out. Speed, Fireball, Red Schwartz, Chris Montague, and Ace Gibbons were right behind him, sucking in great gulps of air. "Who won?" he asked.

"What a question!" Ace gasped. "*You* did! Who'd you think?"

"Got Fireball and me by five yards," Speed managed between gasps of air.

"Beat *you?*"

"Sure!" Fireball agreed. "Speed was second, I was third, Monty was fourth, and Ace was fifth—"

"I wasn't second, Fireball," Speed remonstrated. "You and I crossed the line at the same time."

Chip glanced at Aker and Jacobs and then back to the others in the challenge. Red caught his eye and grinned. "Oh, yes," he whispered, nodding in the direction of the two halfbacks. "The touchdown twins wilted—came in behind Monty, Ace, me, and Gary. Surprise, surprise."

"No!"

"That's right," Speed said.

"Sure!" Ace added grimly. "Cigarettes and hundred-yard challenges don't mix."

"Hey!" Speed interrupted. "Coach Nelson is about to start the centers and guards."

"Mike by ten yards," Ace predicted confidently.

"Uh-uh," Speed disagreed. "Soapy or Anderson."

Chip checked the runners. Mike Brennan could get downfield under punts as fast as anyone. In a game one had to knock blockers out of the way to cover punts, and Mike was an expert at that. But a race was different; it was based on sheer straight-away speed. He looked for Soapy Smith. His lifelong friend was nearly as fast as Speed Morris. Little Eddie Anderson could move too. That left Bebop Leopoulos, Pat O'Malley, Benny Knight, Toby March, and some other players Chip didn't know much about. Soapy was his choice.

Chip was right. Soapy led all the way. Anderson was second and Brennan third. As soon as he crossed the goal line, Soapy turned and swaggered back to join Chip's group. The redhead was breathing heavily, but he had a wide grin on his face. "I'm really a running back," he managed between gulps of air. "I oughta be carrying the ball for the team."

"Tell the coach," Red suggested.

Soapy's blue eyes widened, and the grin faded from his freckled face. "You think I should?" he asked, peering at Red.

"Of course!" Speed interrupted, the back of his hand wiping the perspiration from his face. "You're a real natural!"

"You know the old saying," Red added. "Don't hide your light under a bushel basket."

Ace Gibbons winked at Chip. "Sure, Soapy, tell him!"

"I think I will!" Soapy announced, nodding his head aggressively. "Right now!"

The jovial redhead puffed out his chest for the benefit of his audience and moved purposefully forward. Coach Ralston turned just at that moment. Soapy slowed down, changing his quick stride to a leisurely saunter. Then he glanced at the coach and pivoted swiftly in the opposite direction, but not quite fast enough.

"What is it, Smith?" Ralston asked.

Soapy stopped in his tracks and then slowly turned to face the coach. "I, er, well—" The redhead patted his helmet and shook his head helplessly. "Well, I was thinking that I, er, we were pretty fast coming down the field."

Coach Ralston's sharp eyes shot past Soapy to the smiling group clustered behind the happy-go-lucky guard. He nodded his head vigorously. "You're right. It was a fast race, Smith. Fastest time I've ever seen . . ."

Soapy turned to grin gloatingly toward his pals, but his expression quickly sagged as Coach Ralston finished, ". . . for a bunch of centers and guards!"

Smiling at each other, Coach Ralston and Coach Rockwell watched as the redhead retreated to face the bantering group. Soapy joined in his teammates' laughter just as Coach Nelson started the tackle challenge at midfield.

Biggie Cohen and Joe Maxim were in the lead in the next race. The big linemen matched strides for forty yards, but then Biggie forged ahead to cross the goal line a few feet ahead of Joe. The others were bunched five to ten yards behind them.

"Guess the Valley Falls representatives did all right," Soapy said smugly. "Chip and Speed finish first and second. *And—*" The freckle-faced redhead paused and tried to pat himself on the back. "And good ol' Soapy romps home in first place as usual. Ahem! Biggie duplicates the feat and Red Schwartz—"

"Heads up, now!" Ralston called, walking briskly out in front of the squad. "Not bad, not good! Now it's time we had a little contact work. Coach Nelson has the play cards, and Coach Sullivan will run the defense and their formations. We'll huddle on every play, offense and defense, and work from the cards. I'll watch the offense. Rock, you evaluate the defense." He paused and tossed a ball to Brennan.

"On offense for the first series: Hilton, Finley, Morris, and Gibbons in the backfield; Brennan at center; Smith and Anderson, guards; Cohen and Maxim at tackle; Whittemore and Schwartz, ends.

"On offense for the second series: Young, Jacobs, Roberts, and Aker in the backfield; Leopoulos at center; O'Malley and Knight, guards; Ryan and Logan, tackles; Horton and Montague, ends.

"Coach Sullivan, review the defenses with your groups. You can give Aker and Jacobs a few downs at the linebacker spots too. Coach Nelson, warm up the offensive units at the fifty-yard line. Our scrimmage starts in five minutes."

As the squads moved to their positions on the field, Jack Jacobs caught Travis Aker's eye and declared, "Coach wants to show us off to the rest of these clowns!" Travis nodded in agreement and extended his hand upward for a high-five.

Coach Jim Sullivan had the defensive team set on the twenty-yard line. The offensive team huddled around Coach Nelson and studied the play card he held in his hand.

"Got it?" Chip asked. "All right! Ball on two!"

The card called for one of their favorite plays, a weak-side cross buck. On the count of two, Mike slapped the ball back, and Chip faked to Speed, who was driving over right tackle. Pivoting, Chip then slipped the ball to Fireball and spun out to the right as if to throw a pass. The play was perfectly executed, and Fireball smashed his way through the line and up to the thirty-yard line before two defensive linebackers brought him down.

On the next play, Fireball ran right by Travis Aker, the defensive substitute, brushing him aside as if he wasn't there. Only a desperate dive tackle by Toby March stopped the big fullback from going all the way.

The next card called for a takeoff pass on the previous play. Chip took the ball from Brennan on the count of three, faked to Speed and then Fireball, and cut out to the right behind Soapy, who had pulled out of the line. Then Chip planted his right foot and fired a ten-yard bullet pass to Schwartz, who had buttonhooked back in front of Jacobs. Red pulled in the ball, pivoted, easily evaded Jacobs's weak attempt at a tackle, and picked up five more yards before he was brought down on the forty-five-yard line, again by March.

It wasn't even a good workout for the veterans. They were strong and experienced and had little trouble advancing the ball. After half an hour, Coach Ralston called for one more play, saying, "Finish it up, Nik."

The card Nelson held up for the last play called for an end-around reverse with Whitty carrying the ball. Chip took the ball from Brennan, faked to Speed, and ran along beside Fireball nearly to the line of scrimmage. Then, just as he was about to be tackled, he handed the ball to Schwartz and moved to block Jack Jacobs, who was playing in the defensive left halfback position.

Schwartz cut around to the left side of the line. Whittemore had delayed for a count of four before driving to the right. Red handed the ball to Whitty, and the big end took off around right end. Soapy had pulled out of the line, and he teamed up with Fireball in smearing the first linebacker. Ace Gibbons flattened the end, and only Jacobs was left to stop the big ball carrier.

Jack Jacobs backtracked, his eyes focusing on Whitty's flying legs as he poised gingerly for the tackle. The delay made him an easy target, and Chip took him out with a cross-body block that could be heard clear across the field. Whittemore was away, in the clear, and across the midfield stripe before Ralston's whistle called him back.

Chip had felt a glow of satisfaction as he scrambled to his feet. His had been the key block, and it had been a textbook illustration of the perfect block. But when Jacobs didn't get up, remaining still on the ground, Chip immediately turned to help him.

Jacobs was holding his right leg and glaring at Chip. "You clipped me!" he said angrily between moans. "Got me from behind."

"From behind?" Chip repeated. "How could I? I was right in front of you, right in front of Whitty—"

State University's veteran trainer, Murph Kelly, arrived then and tried to determine the extent of Jacobs's injury. "Stay right there, Jacobs," Kelly said. "Let me have a look."

But Jacobs struggled to his feet and pushed Kelly aside. "Never mind," he muttered. "I'm all right. If Hilton and his clowns want to play dirty football, maybe I can play the same way."

"Take it easy, Jack," Chip said gently. "It was a fair block."

Travis Aker came running up just in time to hear Chip's remark. "Oh, sure!" he said hotly. "Anything *you* do is fair. You're the fair-haired boy around here. How come you never play defense?"

"I can play defense, Aker," Chip said calmly.

"All right, all right," Ralston called. "Break it up! Let Doc Terring take a look at Jacobs, Murph. The rest of you take two laps and hit the showers. Team meeting at eight o'clock."

CHAPTER 3

Jim's Touchdown Twins

COLEMAN "SKIP" MILLER had watched every move his idol made during the scrimmage. When Chip blocked Jacobs out of the play, the young star couldn't restrain his enthusiasm. "What a block!" he cried. "Did you see that, Coach?"

Carpenter nodded. "It was picture perfect, all right," he agreed.

All the fans quieted and remained in their seats while the trainer talked to Jacobs on the field, but not Mr. Jacobs and Mr. Aker.

The two fathers rushed out of the bleachers and hurried across the field before Jack could get to his feet. Jacobs led the way until he reached his son. "What is it, Jack? Your knee?"

Jack Jacobs shook his head. "No, Dad. It's all right."

Mr. Jacobs put his arm around his son's shoulder. "You sure? Let me see you walk."

Jack shrugged his father's arm away and followed Murph Kelly. "I said I'm all right," he said irritably to his father.

"That Hilton shouldn't be allowed to play football," Mr. Aker said angrily, glaring at Chip as he trotted around the field.

Coach Ralston had approached the little group unobserved. "Now, now, Mr. Aker," he chided. "It wasn't Hilton's fault."

Jacobs swung around sharply and looked at Ralston in amazement. "Wasn't Hilton's fault?" he exploded. "Well, whose fault was it?"

"It wasn't anyone's fault," Ralston said evenly. "It was a hard block. This is Division 1 football. It was a good block."

"Block!" Mr. Jacobs repeated incredulously. "You mean a clip! A dirty, vicious clip!"

"You're dead wrong, Mr. Jacobs," Ralston said coolly. "Jack waited too long to make the tackle. Besides, he turned just as Hilton hit him. The block was a good one and perfectly legal. In fact, it was the kind of block I'd like to see every time."

"In a scrimmage? Against a teammate?"

Ralston nodded decisively. "We don't want anyone to get hurt, either in a scrimmage or in a game. But that's why we have scrimmages—to develop hard blocking and tackling. What a player learns in practice is what he'll execute in game situations."

Coach Ralston pivoted and started to walk away, but after a short distance he turned around and retraced his steps. "By the way, gentlemen," he said levelly, "I'll have to ask you to stay off the field."

"But my boy was hurt!"

"I'm sorry about that, Mr. Jacobs. But coming on the field is against football rules. *No* exceptions. Our trainer and the team physician are experts when it comes to athletic injuries."

Ralston walked swiftly away, leaving Jacobs and Aker staring blankly at each other. Aker recovered first. "Well, what do you know," he managed.

The two disgruntled men walked slowly across the field toward the parking area. On the way, they met E. Merton Blaine and his group. "How is your son?" Blaine asked.

"He's all right," Jacobs growled. "A good thing too," he added belligerently. "If he was really hurt, I'd yank him out of State University so fast Ralston's head would swim."

"Yes, and I'd yank Travis right along with him," Mr. Aker added. "It was a clip or I never saw one."

Skip Miller couldn't take that. "It wasn't a clip," he said quickly. "Hilton was *ahead* of the ball carrier. He couldn't have clipped on that play if he had wanted to."

Aker cast a withering glance in Skip's direction. "What do *you* know about football?" he asked sarcastically.

"He knows quite a lot," Coach Carpenter drawled, "enough to be the best high school quarterback in the state."

"What's that got to do with Hilton?" Jacobs asked.

"Nothing," Carpenter said. "But it also happens that I coach football. Hilton's block was not a clip. He fairly blocked your son down from the front as if he were a blocking dummy."

Jacobs glared at Carpenter, his face red with anger. "Another Hilton fan," he said. "I can understand it in kids, but when a man can't see through a . . . a faker like him—"

"Faker is right!" Skip replied cheerfully. "Chip Hilton is the best faking quarterback in the country."

"Come on, you two," Blaine said impatiently. "You're wasting your time."

Other State fans walking slowly across the field to their cars talked about the scrimmage and the team's prospects. All seemed to agree that State had a good first team on offense, but also that the second squad and defense were weak in too many positions.

"He's a good coach, all right, but you can't go through our tough schedule with just an eleven-man team."

"Brown University did it back in my day," an elderly man said.

"Sure, but when was that, Dad? Fifty or sixty years ago?"

"I remember that it was a tougher game back then."

"That may be so, but you know in today's game, one unit can't stand up against four or five well-coached units in the same game. The teams in our conference have talent in every position: an offensive team, a defensive team, a kicking team, and replacements for all of them! We've gotta have more depth."

"Well, all I can say is that Coach Curly Ralston's got himself a problem."

"You mean a lot of problems!"

After dinner, Coach Ralston and his assistants, Rockwell, Nelson, and Sullivan, gathered in the living room of the coaches' cabin.

"Well," Ralston said cryptically, "I thought maybe Jacobs and Hilton—"

"Chip is too smart for that," Nelson said quietly. "Besides, I don't think Jacobs has the guts to start a fight with anyone."

Sullivan snorted in disgust. "Humph. Touchdown twins!"

"What are we going to do with them?" Ralston asked.

"Cut them from the squad," Sullivan suggested shortly. "They spell trouble for the rest of the team."

There was a long silence and then Ralston continued. "I don't understand it. Aker and Jacobs played good football with our freshman team. What happened?"

Sullivan shifted restlessly in his chair. "They didn't have any competition for one thing," he said. "Besides, they're showboats and have developed an overinflated view of their skills."

"They're more than showboats," Coach Henry Rockwell said slowly. "They're big and fast and they played some good offensive and defensive football with the freshman team. Personally, I think they are handicapped by their fathers."

"There's no question about that," Ralston said, shaking his head ruefully. He spread his hands helplessly. "Well, Rock, what do you suggest?"

"Hang onto them, Curly. They might fool us and grow up. But they'll have to be brought along slowly."

"What about the training rules?" Nelson demanded. "You saw them die in the race this afternoon."

"Let Murph handle it," Ralston suggested. "I'll speak to him." He glanced at his watch and rose slowly to his feet. "Well, it's time for the meeting. Let's go."

When they reached the assembly hall, Nik Nelson and Jim Sullivan rolled in the white board, and Henry Rockwell arranged the chairs. Curly Ralston's assistants were specialists and tops in their fields. Nelson and Sullivan were State graduates, loved their alma mater, and worked hard at their jobs. Nelson was small, quick, and impulsive. Sullivan was tall, heavy, and powerful. Both were enthusiastic, loyal, and cooperative, and both lived and breathed football.

Henry Rockwell was a veteran of many years of football coaching. He was compactly built, strong, and quick in his movements. His black hair and upright carriage gave him the appearance of a much younger man.

Rockwell had coached at Valley Falls High School until he reached retirement age. Then he had accepted a position in the athletic department at State University, where he served as assistant football coach. Like his former high school players, Chip, Soapy, Biggie, Speed, and Red, he was starting his third year at State. He was a keen student of football and a shrewd tactician. Curly Ralston depended greatly upon his advice and judgment.

Murph Kelly was already calling the team roll when Jacobs and Aker casually strolled into the room. "All present, Coach," he said, staring at the two latecomers.

Ralston moved to the board and drew a number of circles on its surface. "We'll start using this huddle on Monday," he said, turning to face the players. "As you can see, I've placed it close to the line of scrimmage, two yards from the ball. This will limit the time the defense has to send in subs and get organized. However, we will also use it as a deep huddle, seven to ten yards from the ball.

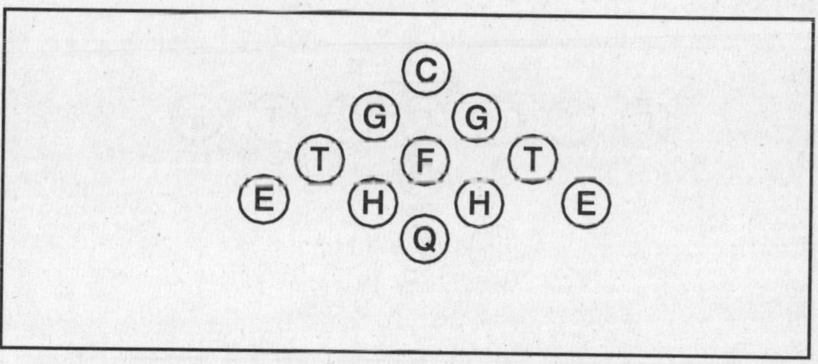

"Everyone faces away from the ball except the quarterback. The fullback kneels in the center of the huddle and everyone else places his hands on his thighs. Any questions?"

"How about the signals?" Fireball asked.

"I'll get to those in a minute, Finley. With respect to the huddle, when we're close to the line, we'll use the numbered plays and snap count and the quarterback will call them out. Keep in mind that this close position will be used when we want to move quickly into position and get our play off before the opponents can shift their defensive positions to meet our strength. Naturally, when we're in the deeper position, we'll use our established signals and play numbers. Everyone get it?"

As there were no further questions concerning the huddle, Coach Ralston then spent a full hour discussing the play signals and check signals. Then he dismissed the squad.

After the players left, Rockwell, Nelson, and Sullivan moved to the front of the room, and Ralston turned and drew a standard offense formation on the board.

Then he sat down on the edge of the desk. "Let's talk a little about personnel and positions," he said, tossing the marker to Nelson. "Write the names on the board, Nik. Brennan at center; Smith and Anderson, guards; Cohen and Maxim, tackles; Whittemore and Schwartz, ends. Finley, Morris, and Gibbons, running backs; Hilton, quarterback."

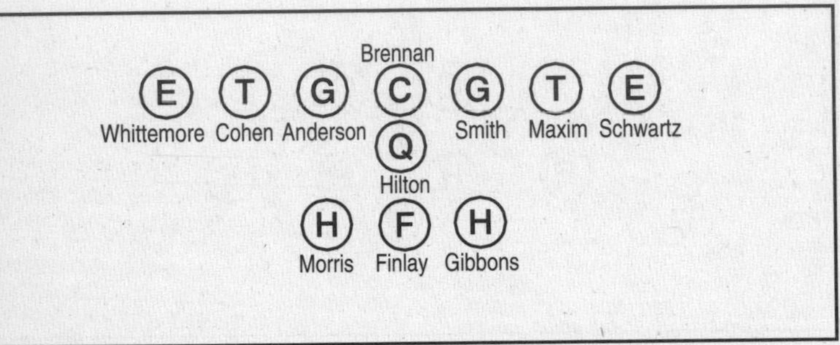

"No question about Brennan," Sullivan said, starting it off. "Mike's the best center in the conference. Six feet in height, 200 pounds, and as hard as they come."

"How about the guards?" Ralston asked.

"Smith is all right," Nelson answered, "but Anderson is too small."

Rockwell nodded. "Right. We've got to find another guard somewhere. Anderson plays with a lot of heart and makes a good sub on offense. He might make a strong defensive player, but we need a bigger guard to stand up under the pressure from our opponents."

"No argument about the tackles," Sullivan said. "Biggie Cohen is the fastest big man I ever saw. He and Maxim are good enough to go pro right now."

Ralston smiled. "You're sold on those two, aren't you? All right, Rock, what about the ends?"

Rockwell studied the names on the board. "Whittemore should be due for a great year. Six-four, 210, fast—"

"And the best pass receiver on the squad," Nelson finished for him.

"Schwartz might also be one of our better ends," Rockwell continued, "but I think Montague ought to be given a lot of consideration."

"He's pretty light though," Nelson said. "Six-three and only 160 pounds."

Ralston nodded his agreement. "How about the backfield?"

Sullivan grinned. "Are you kidding? How could it be improved?"

"It's got everything," Nelson said. "Hilton is an all-American quarterback. He can run, pass, kick, and is a coach on the field. Morris is as fleet and savvy a halfback as you'll ever see. Finley is a blockbusting fullback, and Gibbons is also a great blocker."

"Remember a year ago?" Ralston mused. "We broke up a senior team to include a sophomore bunch—"

"And," Nelson interrupted, "won the conference championship."

"Right!" Sullivan agreed. "But that was last year. Those players have graduated and *they*—"

He paused and tapped the table significantly. "And *they* gave us the experienced offensive and defensive depth a championship team needs. This year . . ."

He paused again and shrugged his shoulders expressively. "This year we've got three seniors and eight juniors on that starting offensive line and not a lot to back them up."

"No team can afford to lose sixteen lettermen from their offense and expect to have any depth the following year," Nelson said. "We'll be in a real mess if a couple of our key starters get hurt."

"We have a fine offensive team," Rockwell said, speaking thoughtfully. "Good enough to give us plenty of scoring strength—"

"But—" Ralston prompted.

"But," Rockwell continued, "we can't keep the ball all the time. When we don't have it, we'll be in trouble. It's the defense that gives me the most concern."

"What do you suggest?" Ralston asked.

The veteran coach deliberated briefly. "Well," Rockwell said thoughtfully, "I think we should change our offense. We could open it up and build it around Chip."

"That's no problem," Ralston said softly. "Go on."

"And," Rockwell continued grimly, "I think we've got to shift Morris and Gibbons to defense and then consider having Brennan, Cohen, Maxim, and Schwartz put in quality work on both sides of the line."

"I can't see that," Nelson said quickly, shaking his head. "Chip wouldn't have anyone to work with."

"Right!" Sullivan agreed. "Why kill a good offense?"

Ralston held up a hand. "Hold it, men. Rock has the floor." He turned back to Rockwell. "Who would you put in the backfield to replace Morris and Gibbons?"

Rockwell glanced at Jim Sullivan and smiled. "Jim's touchdown twins," he said gently. "Aker and Jacobs."

CHAPTER 4

Surprises to the Playbook

TRAINER MURPH KELLY surprised everyone Monday morning at breakfast when he announced that a team meeting would be substituted for the usual group work. "Nine-thirty in the lecture room," the trainer said. "Shorts and T-shirts."

Chip and his Valley Falls friends—Soapy, Speed, Red, and Biggie—were sharing a table with Fireball and Whitty. When Kelly finished his announcement, Soapy pushed his plate away, leaned back in his chair, and sighed happily. "I'm beginning to love this training camp," he drawled. "Now all we need is breakfast in bed."

"It won't last," Chip warned. "Coach has something on his mind."

"He has his troubles and I have mine," Soapy said loftily.

"Sure!" Speed agreed. "We know—food and sleep!"

"Uh-uh," Soapy said, shaking his head and pursing his lips. "My only trouble is Mitzi."

Whitty winked at Speed. "That reminds me," he said thoughtfully, "I owe her a letter."

Soapy's blue eyes opened wide, and he swung his head around in surprise. "You mean she wrote you a letter?"

Whitty nodded gravely. "She sure did. Told me about Mr. Grayson and the guys who took over our jobs at the counter this summer and—"

"She say anything about me?" Soapy interrupted.

"Nope, not a word."

A pained expression shot across Soapy's face. "I don't understand it," he moaned.

"You shouldn't have gone to Asia," Whitty said helpfully. "You know the old saying: Out of sight, out of mind."

"But I *had* to go with the ball club," Soapy moaned forlornly.

"Oh, yeah," Whitty continued. "She did ask about Chip. She said the stockroom was a mess, and it would take him a month to straighten it out."

"You said Mitzi was going out with one of those summer replacement guys, didn't you?" Fireball asked casually.

"Well," Whitty hesitated, glancing in Soapy's direction, "that's what she said."

Soapy had been fidgeting restlessly in his chair. Now he glanced at his watch. "Oh, no!" he said, leaping to his feet. "I gotta go!"

"Where are you going?" Fireball asked. "What's the rush?"

"I, er, well, I gotta make a phone call to Grayson's. A *business* call!"

"Mitzi usually takes all of Mr. Grayson's calls," Whitty suggested. "Or hadn't you thought of that?"

"I thought of it, *all right,*" Soapy said gravely, hurrying away from the table.

As soon as Soapy was out of earshot, the rest of the table erupted into laughter. "He thought of it!" Whitty cried. "C'mon! This is one phone conversation I've got to hear."

An hour later when the players gathered in the lecture room, Soapy took a seat as far away from his breakfast club friends as possible. But he couldn't avoid their amused glances. Chip was getting a big kick out of the joke. He knew Soapy through and through, and the lovable redhead wasn't kidding him. Soapy was putting on a great act for his buddies; he had known from the beginning that it was all a joke.

Ralston waited until the players quieted and then moved to his usual position against the desk. "Men," he said, "while you were taking it easy over the weekend, your coaching staff has been hard at work." He paused to let that sink in and then went on. "Just about this time a year ago, we had a big squad with plenty of depth in every position. Still, we were faced with a difficult decision."

Ralston walked slowly around the table and then continued, "That decision called for the breaking up of an experienced offensive team mostly comprised of seniors. We shifted the veterans to a defensive unit and replaced them with a bunch of talented sophomores.

"That gave us a fine combination: a fast, high-scoring offensive team and a solid core of defensive veterans who made up an experienced and strong defensive platoon. It worked out fine.

"Now, just one year later, we're faced with almost the same problem. This time, however, we're in a different position. We have a veteran offensive team, but only a few replacements. And more importantly, we don't have enough experienced players to form a strong, competitive defensive platoon."

Chip was sitting between Speed and Soapy and felt his two teammates grow tense. Ralston had left a lot hanging in the air.

"So," Ralston continued, "we have no alternative. We're going to split up the squad and move some of our offensive regulars to the defensive platoon. Coach Nelson has copies of the changes for each of you to put into your playbooks."

There was a buzz of excitement among the players, but they quieted down when Coach Ralston held up his hand for silence. "That isn't all," he said. "We're discarding last year's offense for a new one, *and* we're adopting a new defensive system."

That statement brought a murmur of surprise, but the players quieted as the determined coach continued. "Since we have a fairly young team from a depth perspective, every player here must master his respective offensive or defensive changes. Some of you upperclassmen can expect additional playing time on both sides of the ball.

"That also means some of the younger players can expect additional playing responsibilities at key positions. We'll go over the defense later. You're excused for the rest of the morning. Study the formations and plays, and we'll try to clear up any questions you may have this afternoon."

Chip and his Valley Falls pals, along with Fireball Finley and Whitty Whittemore, had managed to get a cabin together. They walked slowly in that direction, each member of the group engrossed in the playbook additions he carried.

"Offensive team," Soapy said, reading the names. "Leopoulos, center; O'Malley and Smith, guards; Ryan and Logan, tackles; Whittemore and Montague, ends. Backfield: Hilton, Finley, Aker, and Jac—" He stopped dead in his tracks. "*Aker* and *Jacobs!*"

"Cut it out, Soapy. That isn't even funny," Red exclaimed.

"Honest, I'm reading straight from the playbook." Soapy gestured to the open page.

"No way!" Fireball exploded. "You mean Chip and I are gonna have to put up with those two in the backfield?"

"That's what it says," Whittemore said grimly.

"No way!" Fireball said again hotly. "As of right now, I'm going to ask to be assigned to the defensive squad!"

"Who's gonna do the blocking?" Red asked.

"I know who's gonna do the talking," Soapy said. "Chip and Fireball will have to wear earplugs in the huddle."

"It won't be that bad," Chip protested.

"Oh, no?" Speed challenged. "Wait and see, man."

They had reached the cabin now, and Chip changed the subject. "How do you like the new formation?" he asked, spreading the paper out on the table.

"It's sure different," Fireball commented. "They've sure opened it up."

"Opened it up is right," Chip murmured.

"Mixed it up is more like it," Soapy grumbled. "You ever see such a crazy mixed-up formation?"

"It's not crazy, Soapy," Chip soothed. "I've seen Oklahoma use it, and they've been doing all right on the offense for years."

"The left halfback is playing right end when the line is unbalanced to the right," Speed observed. "What's the idea with that?"

"It sets him up for passes, I guess," Chip ventured.

"I think it gives the end a better blocking position," Red suggested.

"The fullback is two yards behind the line, and the halfback is five yards back," Fireball said thoughtfully. "That means the quarterback has to do some quick ballhandling on the dive plays."

"That won't be a problem," Whitty said. "Chip'll take care of that."

"He'll have to take care of more than the dive plays," Biggie said. "This new offense is built around the quarterback position. He can use the quarterback sneak, feed the fullback or the halfback on the dive plays, or fake to them and keep the ball."

"That means Chip will be running the ball a lot," Speed added.

Fireball nodded. "And doing a lot of passing," he added.

"Hey, you know what? I like it," Whitty said.

"How about you, Chip? What do you think?" Biggie asked.

"I don't know," Chip answered thoughtfully, checking the spacing of the linemen. "It'll definitely spread the defense."

"It looks to me as if it's more for running than passing," said Fireball. "The coach said the fullback and the halfback drive for the line as soon as the ball is passed."

"That ought to help the passing attack," Chip said. "Since the fullback and halfback are driving forward, that means the defensive line will be concentrating on them instead of the quarterback. Besides, the pass receivers are spread clear across the field. Look at this!"

Turning the paper over, Chip quickly sketched several passing alleys for the receivers.

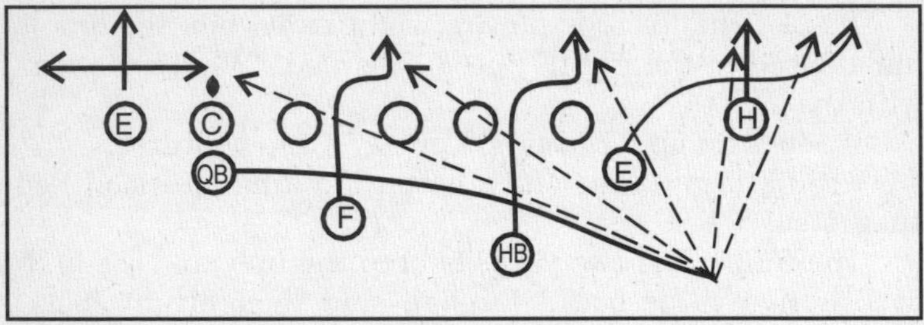

"Chip's right," Red observed. "I'll bet Coach Ralston has all kinds of pass patterns worked out."

"But he didn't give you many plays," Fireball added, flipping through the pages of his red notebook.

"That's what gives the formation strength," Speed concluded.

"This has the potential to be a better system than we had last season," Biggie declared. "All it takes is for everybody to know their stuff and execute their assignments."

Chip and his friends spent the rest of the morning studying and discussing the new formation and plays. When they reported for practice that afternoon, they understood the new formation and its objectives. They all agreed that their coaches had done what was best for the team—even if it meant individual players had to learn more variations to the game of football.

"All right," Ralston called right after the last drill finished, "offensive squad over here. Defensive squad report to Coach Rockwell. Let's go, Hilton. You're over the ball, Leopoulos."

Assistant Coach Nelson had the play cards ready, and Chip studied the first one while he waited for his offensive teammates to form behind the ball. Then he faced the huddle, noting that only Whitty, Soapy, and Fireball remained from the offensive team that had upset A & M for the conference championship the previous year.

Two hours later Chip sighed in relief when Coach Ralston blasted his whistle and called it a day. And what a day it had been! He and Fireball waited for Soapy and Whitty before the four of them took their cool-down laps together. Biggie, Speed, and Red cut across the field and joined them.

"How did it go?" Speed asked curiously.

"All right," Chip said lightly.

Soapy laughed cynically. "Yeah right! That's a laugh! If you can call bumping heads, running through the wrong holes, complaining about the way Chip handled the ball and—"

"And trying to run the team," Fireball growled. "I've met a lot of phonies, but those two guys take the gold medal. Every time either Aker or Jacobs made a mistake, they had an excuse."

"And *talk!*" Whittemore added. "Chip couldn't get a word in edgewise in the huddle."

"We'll see who does the talking Wednesday afternoon," Biggie said ominously.

Wednesday, after a short morning practice, Chip and Soapy took a long, leisurely hike around Camp Sundown, gradually working the tightness and soreness out of their muscles. As soon as they were out of earshot, Soapy brought up the subject uppermost in their thoughts. "Well," he said, "it won't be long now. How do you think this new offense will go?"

"The offense is all right," Chip said, "but—"

"But you don't think we can do much against Biggie and Maxim and Red and the rest of them. Right?"

"That's right," Chip said grimly. "There's something missing."

"What?"

"Offensive unity, spirit, harmony, a lot of things. Essential things."

Soapy shook his head disapprovingly. "You ought to tell those two guys where to get off," he said bitterly.

"They aren't my responsibility, Soapy."

"But they keep riding you, trash-talking, making dirty digs! *I* wouldn't take it."

"Soapy, you know I'm not interested in what they say."

"Well, I'm surprised Ralston and Nelson can't see through their nonsense."

"Coach knows what he's doing, Soapy."

"He's sure keeping everyone else in the dark."

"What do you mean?" Chip asked.

"I mean keeping those two guys on the offensive team. And moving them into starting spots. Why? What for?"

"Maybe we'll find out this afternoon."

Soapy grunted. "Humph! They haven't shown me a thing. Except that they're whiners and complainers."

"Maybe they're not practice players."

"Maybe they're not players. Period!"

CHAPTER 5

Quite a Backfield

GEE-GEE GRAY shuffled several papers in his hands and grinned across the table at Chip Hilton and Skip Miller. The only sound in the room was the soft purr of the broadcasting equipment the technicians had set up in the main building at Camp Sundown.

Chip glanced at the young high school star, noting the blond hair, gray eyes, and determined chin. Now that he'd had a chance to study the teenager, Chip had to admit that there was definitely a strong resemblance. It gave him a strange feeling. For a moment he thought about his mom and wondered what her expression would be the first time she saw Skip Miller. Chip thought he must have looked like Skip three years ago when he was a senior in high school. . . . Then, Gee-Gee Gray's voice cut through his musing.

"Hi, sports fans. Welcome to WSUN 1100. You're listening to the station that brings you State University football. This is Gee-Gee Gray bringing you a special football preview from Camp Sundown, State University's football training camp. This morning I had a chance to visit with the coaching staff.

I even had a long talk with Coach Curly Ralston about some of this year's players and about State's prospects for the upcoming season.

"Right now, I want you to meet two great quarterbacks," Gray said, winking at his two guests before continuing. "Sitting in front of me here at Camp Sundown is State University's all-American field general, Chip Hilton. And right beside him is Skip Miller, our very own University High School all-state quarterback.

"I feel like I'm talking to clones! These two great athletes look enough alike to be brothers. Both have blond hair, gray eyes, and tanned complexions. Skip looks like a slightly smaller version of Chip! Hilton stands just over six-four and tips the scales at 190 pounds.

"First, Chip Hilton! Chip, this is the first time we've had a chance to talk to you about football since you were selected for the all-America team. Can you tell our listeners how you felt when the Associated Press, the United Press International, the National Collegiate Football Coaches Association, and just about every sportswriter in the country named you to their teams?"

Chip glanced ruefully at Skip and shook his head in resignation. "Well, Mr. Gray, I was completely surprised and very happy. I didn't expect it and I don't think I deserved it, since there is still much I have to learn about this game. I hope I can play well this season and try to make good on the honor."

"You're being a little too modest, Chip Hilton, but we'll let you get away with it. Now, what about this year's State team? How does it compare with last year's championship squad?"

"It's pretty early to say, Mr. Gray. We have a lot of new players out for the team who show great promise and determination, but we lost some very solid lettermen from last year's team. Besides, we haven't had a good scrimmage game yet—"

"You've got an intrasquad scrimmage this afternoon and a practice game with Wesleyan on Saturday, haven't you?"

"Yes, sir. That ought to give us a pretty good idea."

Gray laughed. "Thank you, Chip. It was a great pleasure to have you visit with us on this special football segment. And we hope you'll join us for some postgame shows as the season progresses.

"Yes, I think all you State football fans would agree it looks as if Coach Curly Ralston is going to have himself quite a backfield with an all-American at quarterback, a set of touchdown twins in the halfback slots, and a veteran fullback to round it out."

Gray grinned across the table at Skip Miller. "Now we're going to hear from the younger version of my first guest. I want you to meet our own home-grown, hometown star, the great high school football player who gave University High a state championship and won all-state honors for himself: Skip Miller.

"Skip, this is *your* first appearance on our program since last fall, isn't it?"

Skip nodded nervously. "Yes, sir. Yes, sir, it is."

"Now, Skip, is it really true that all your teammates call you Skip *Hilton?* How do you feel about that?"

Skip glanced at Chip and smiled. "I like it," he said firmly. "I try to play just like he does." Then he added quickly, "Not that I can ever do it as well as he does."

"Coach Carpenter tells me you've patterned your style of play after Chip's. What does he mean by that?"

"Well, sir, Coach Carpenter used the same formation last year that State used, and I watched Chip in the practices and games. I tried to, well, I tried to imitate him." Skip paused and then continued hastily. "Not that I can come close, but, well, I try."

"You must think a lot of the way Chip Hilton plays football then."

Skip nodded his head vigorously. “I sure do. He’s the greatest!”

Gray smiled warmly. “You’re a great quarterback, too, Skip Miller. And you’re on the right track. You just keep right on imitating Chip Hilton.

“Now, one last question. You don’t have to answer unless you want to. I know there have been college scouts and recruiters contacting you. A lot of University and State fans are wondering—me, too—where you plan to go to college next year.”

Skip hesitated, and it seemed to Chip that he glanced at him for help. Then the boy shook his head uncertainly and chose his words carefully. “I don’t know, Mr. Gray. I can’t make up my mind between State and Brand University. My uncle—”

“I know, Skip,” Gray interrupted. “Your uncle is an alumnus of Brand University, and he wants you to play for his alma mater. That’s understandable. However, I’m sure all the State fans join me in hoping you’ll stay right here in University.

“Thanks for joining us on this short State University football segment. Be sure to join us this evening for our regular sports program. After this short break, I’ll be right back for some final thoughts. Stay with us.”

The sportscaster gestured toward the door. “Thanks, Skip. We’ll be watching you on the gridiron this fall. Good luck to both of you great quarterbacks.”

Gray continued with his broadcast as Chip and Skip tiptoed out of the room. “Everyone is at lunch, Skip,” Chip commented. “I never eat lunch before a hard scrimmage or a game.”

Skip shrugged his shoulders. “That’s all right. We ate on the way down. Anyway, I’m not hungry.” He hesitated a second and then continued. “Chip, I’d like to talk football with you if you have time. I need some advice.”

Chip laughed. "I have lots of time, Skip. But I don't know about the advice part. What's on your mind?"

"It's about college. You heard what I said to Gee-Gee Gray about State and Brand?"

"Sure, but where do *you* want to go?"

"I'd like to go to State."

"Why don't you?"

"It's a little hard to explain. Uncle Merton is worth a lot of money, and he's president of his own company. Dad works for him. . . ." Skip spread his hands helplessly. "Besides, he's been awfully good to me. And I like him."

"How about your mom and dad? How do they feel about it?"

"That's the trouble. Dad works for Uncle Merton, and he and Mom don't want to, well, they don't want to go against his wishes."

"Why is your uncle so set on Brand?"

"Well, for one thing, he and the coach are friends. Besides, Uncle Merton is chairman of the Brand Alumni Association."

Chip nodded thoughtfully. "That does make it tough."

"You can say that again," Skip agreed. "I don't exactly know how to put it into words, Chip, but my dad hasn't been too successful in business. He doesn't have a college education or a trade, and as he reminds me, he's not young. If Uncle Merton got upset for some reason and Dad lost his job . . . . Well, I kinda feel that I'm making a college decision not just for me but for my entire family."

"Do you think your uncle would be that unreasonable?"

"I've heard he's got a pretty mean temper when someone in business crosses him. And I'm sure my parents couldn't afford to send me to college without Uncle Merton's help."

"But you wouldn't be any expense to your parents if you were at State," Chip explained. "You'd probably get an athletic scholarship, or you could work. I work! I'm sure my boss would give you a job."

"Where do you work, Chip?"

"You know Grayson's, don't you? At Tenth and State. You must be the only high schooler in town who doesn't know where it is."

"Sure, I know where it is! I go in sometimes. I've seen Soapy, Finley, and Whitty Whittemore working, but I've never seen you there."

"That's because I work in the stockroom."

They came to Chip's cabin, and the two boys sat down on the bench on the porch. Skip had been absorbed in thought. He cleared his throat nervously. "You really think your boss would give me a job?" he asked.

"I can ask him, Skip. You're sure you want a job?"

"Absolutely! Just try me! I'll do anything!"

Their conversation was interrupted by the voices of the players walking back from the dining room. "I'll see you again this Saturday," Skip said happily. "That is, if it's all right—"

"I'll be glad to see you any time. Are you staying to watch the intrasquad scrimmage?"

"I wouldn't miss it!" Skip replied, grinning back over his shoulder.

Before Chip's friends reached their cottage, Murph Kelly blasted his whistle. "All right!" he yelled, his voice carrying clearly to all sides of the small clearing. "Everyone hit the rack and relax, and no gabbing! And I mean *now!* Taping at 2:30! The student trainers will be at the field. Practice begins at three! All of you know to be on time!"

Chip crawled thankfully into his bunk to relax. He wanted all the rest he could get before the scrimmage. He dozed off, and it seemed only a few minutes later when Kelly's siren sounded. Chip dressed in the cabin and walked alone down the walkway leading from the cabins to the practice field. At the sideline, he reviewed the new plays again while a senior student trainer taped his ankles. Snapping the playbook closed, Chip confidently walked onto the field.

"Look at the crowd," Soapy gasped.

Chip led the squad through their warm-up exercises, and then Coach Ralston named the offensive and defensive teams. "No punches pulled this afternoon," he said crisply. "Offensive team take the ball on the twenty. Defensive team take it away from them! Let's go!"

Chip dropped twelve yards behind the ball and looked at the defensive formation. It gave him a strange feeling to see Biggie, Maxim, Brennan, Gibbons, Schwartz, and Morris facing him on the other side of the ball.

"All right, guys," Chip began. "They're setting up in a 5-4-2 defense, practically a nine-man line. That's an open invitation for passes, but we'll run a few times to get everyone in game mode. Heads up, now! Right formation! Fifty-five on three! That's you, Aker, straight ahead. Right after I fake to Fireball, you'll get the ball. Got it?"

"I know the plays," Aker said sharply. "You call 'em and I'll run 'em. That's all you've got to do."

Chip called, "Break!" and clapped his hands, and then the team strode up to the line of scrimmage. Leopoulos plunked the ball back on the "three" count, and Chip faked to Fireball, but Aker was slow getting started off the mark. Chip had to wait for the surly halfback. He slipped the ball under Aker's arms and continued on out and back as if to make a pass.

Aker didn't even get back to the line of scrimmage. Biggie Cohen smashed through the line, met the sophomore head-on, lifted him off the ground, and smacked him down on his back five yards behind the line. Biggie then got to his feet, reached down, and picked Aker up as gently as if he were a baby. "Sorry, buddy," he drawled. "Just part of the game."

"Nobody blocked you!" Aker snarled. "No wonder you got through."

"You're right," Biggie said blandly. "Come back and see me again sometime. I'll be right here."

Grumbling and griping, Aker limped back to the huddle. “C’mon, Logan, Montague,” he said angrily. “What’s the idea? Let’s block somebody next time.”

“Cut the chatter!” Chip said sharply. “Quarterback runs the huddle.”

“He’s right, Travis,” Jacobs said, shaking a finger at his buddy. “When the great Hilton talks, no one, but no one, is supposed to even breathe.”

“Formation left,” Chip said coolly. “Thirty-six on two!”

“Don’t tell me now!” Jacobs said nastily. “That means I hit straight ahead on the count of two, right?”

No one answered. Chip’s “Break!” sent the team out of the huddle and up to the line. “Hut one, hut two—”

Chip faked to Fireball and handed the ball to Jacobs. This time, Joe Maxim drove through the line. But he didn’t tackle Jacobs; he simply lifted his powerful forearm, catching Jack across the chest. Jack was stopped instantly. He had run into the Maxim wall! Jacobs’s head snapped backward, and the ball popped forward out of his soft hands.

“My, my!” Mike Brennan said cheerfully, falling on the ball. “What have we here? Looky what I found! Anybody lose something?”

“All right!” Coach Ralston called. “Offensive team again. Some offense! Two plays and we lose five yards on one play and the ball on the other.” He turned to nod toward the defensive team. “Nice going, Cohen, Maxim, and Brennan. Pour it on ’em!”

Back in the huddle, Jacobs was complaining bitterly. “What kind of football is this? That Maxim didn’t even try to tackle me. He hit me with his fists.”

“Quiet!” Chip barked. “Formation left! Twenty-two on one! Break!”

Chip made his snap count, and Fireball smashed through O’Malley and Roberts for seven yards. Back in the huddle, Chip thumped Fireball on the back. “Nice goin’, Fireball. That gave them something to think about!”

"Cut out the bouquets and call the plays!" Aker growled.

"Now, now, Travis," Jacobs snipped, "remember, quarterback runs the huddle."

"Formation right," Chip said, ignoring the remarks. "Nineteen on three. Break!"

This time, Chip faked to Fireball and then to Aker, keeping the ball himself. The "keeper" was one of his favorite plays, but it required particularly good faking on the part of the halfback. Fireball faked beautifully, slipping his arms over the ball and driving into the line for all he was worth, but Aker barely went through the motions. Red and Biggie nailed Chip at the line of scrimmage.

"Surprise, surprise," Jacobs said when they were back in the huddle. "You see that, Travis? Hilton must have forgotten to tell his buddies to step aside."

"They knew I was coming," Chip said evenly. "You told them, Travis."

"Me?"

"Yes, *you!* You didn't even half fake carrying the ball. None of our plays are going to be any good if we don't work together."

"How come you didn't say anything when they stopped Travis and me?" Jacobs asked.

"That's right!" Aker added. "They stop you once and you start whining."

"*Whining!*" Soapy repeated, pushing roughly through the huddle. "That's all you two guys have been doing. Whining and bragging and bluffing—"

"What's going on here?" Coach Ralston demanded.

CHAPTER 6

Huddle Lawyers

COACH RALSTON'S face was flushed, and his voice was sharp and bitter. He walked into the middle of the huddle, hands clenched, jaw set, eyes snapping. "I asked what's going on here," he repeated.

There was no reply as he glared around the circle of faces. On the other side of the ball, the defensive players remained quietly in place, absorbed in Ralston's words.

"All right! Then I'll tell you what was going on! For one thing, we had three quarterbacks trying to run a team that doesn't know its plays. For another thing, the huddle sounded like a bunch of snarling, yapping puppies. And we had a couple of would-be ball carriers whining because they got clobbered when they carried the ball.

"Now you listen to me! All of you!" He turned to face the defensive squad and pointed his finger at them. "And this includes you!" He paused and there was dead silence. Then he motioned for the defensive players to come forward. When they had circled him, he continued. "I don't like to take scrimmage time for a lecture, but this has gone far enough."

Ralston stopped and glared at Junior Roberts, who had dropped to one knee. "And *you!*" he barked. "You get up on your feet! When you play for State, for me, for yourself, you're always on your feet unless you're hurt! You understand that?"

Roberts scrambled hastily to his feet, his face almost as red as Coach Ralston's. "Yes, sir!" he gasped. "Yes, sir!"

"All right! For the last time! The offensive quarterback runs the offensive team. The defensive linebacker runs the defensive team. *Is that clear?* No ifs, ands, or buts! In the offensive huddle I want absolute silence. Why? Well, I suppose I'll have to tell some of you practicing *huddle lawyers* why.

"In the first place, the quarterback is the pivotal player on the team. *He* runs the show! He's the communication link between his unit on the field, his team on the sidelines, and the entire coaching staff. It's up to him to call the right play, to decide when to gamble and when to play it safe. He is expected to spot our opponents' weaknesses and exploit them; he has to memorize a hundred plays and be able to call the right play for the right situation. And he has to know his own plays as well as those of every other player on the team.

"When it comes to making a decision for running the ball, passing, or handing off the ball, the quarterback is on his own, with no question or suggestion from anyone! The success of the running attack rests not only upon his ability to call the right play but also upon his astuteness in concealing the intent by clever faking and maneuvering."

Ralston paused and scanned the circle of faces. Not a player moved. When the tall mentor continued, his voice had lost much of its edge, but it was obvious he was still upset.

"Now, all of the planning and faking and maneuvering by the quarterback is useless—I repeat *useless*—unless he gets the cooperation of *every* player on the team. When the quarterback fakes to give the ball to a back, that back must run just as hard as if he actually had the ball. A fake is not a fake unless it looks like the real thing. I want it to look so real that it fools opponents, officials, coaches, and even the spectators in the top row of the stadium.

"Chip Hilton is an expert at handling the ball. I often stand behind the defensive team just to see if I can follow the ball and spot the actual carrier. He fools me consistently, time after time, often when I know the play.

"That isn't all. The quarterback in our style of play has to make 90 percent of the passes. He has to make them on the run, standing still, or off balance. And he has to get the ball away with five or six opponents chasing him or hanging on his neck. He's not expected to eat the ball either. That means he's not supposed to hold onto the ball and get thrown for a big loss.

"One last thing. We spend countless hours with our quarterbacks in private strategy sessions. Hours of tedious study and discussion in which game situations and problems are reviewed time after time. It should be obvious that the quarterback needs—no, must have—quiet in the huddle. He must not be disturbed by senseless bickering or suggestions, *especially* in the huddle. All right! Let's try it again."

Chip called the next play, and the team ran up to the line, conscious that Ralston's eyes were on their every move. Chip took the ball from Leopoulos and faked to Fireball. Then he continued to the left along the line and faked to Jacobs. Holding the ball on his hip, he cut around and picked up six yards.

Ralston waited until the players had sprinted to their huddle positions. "Same shift," he said briskly. "A buttonhook pass to Whittemore. Ball on three!"

"Let's go!" Fireball barked.

"We'll kill 'em!" Soapy yelped enthusiastically. "C'mon, you guys! Run over 'em!"

Finally, there was a real snap in the execution of the play. It started off like a repeat of the keeper, but after faking to

Fireball and Jacobs, Chip cut back and dug his right foot into the turf. Aker, playing the offensive left-end position on the shift to the left, broke straight down and then cut toward the center of the field. Whittemore, playing a yard behind the line, followed Aker for ten yards and then buttonhooked back. Chip fired the ball into the big athlete's numbers on the midfield stripe. Whitty pivoted and made three more yards before Speed Morris dropped him on the forty-seven-yard line.

"Nice pitching!" Whitty chirped, plunking the ball down and hustling back to the huddle.

Ralston had followed the play and was waiting once more when the huddle formed. "Double reverse!" he said sharply. "Formation right. Hilton fakes to Finley and Aker and gives the ball to Montague. Montague runs left and hands the ball to Whittemore for the second part of the reverse around right end. On three. Got it?"

There was no reply before Chip's "Break!" sent them out of the huddle and up to the line in a spirited rush. On the "three" count Leopoulos centered the ball, and Chip faked to Fireball and then Aker before slipping the ball to Montague. Continuing his fake, Chip cut off-tackle and headed for Speed Morris, who was playing defensive left halfback.

Chip had no chance to see the play develop, but he knew something had gone wrong when Speed backed away from his block and fended him off with his hands. He turned on the whistle and saw Biggie and Roberts lifting Whitty to his feet. The big end had been thrown for a five-yard loss. Chip hurried back to the huddle. "What happened?" he asked.

"Cohen happened!" Whitty rasped. "No one touched him!"

"Simmer down, Whittemore," Ralston said coolly. He turned to Nelson. "Let me have the play, Nik."

Nelson handed the big play card to Ralston. He laid it on the grass and knelt down in front of it to explain the play. "There are four key blocks," he said, pointing to the card. "I'll explain them.

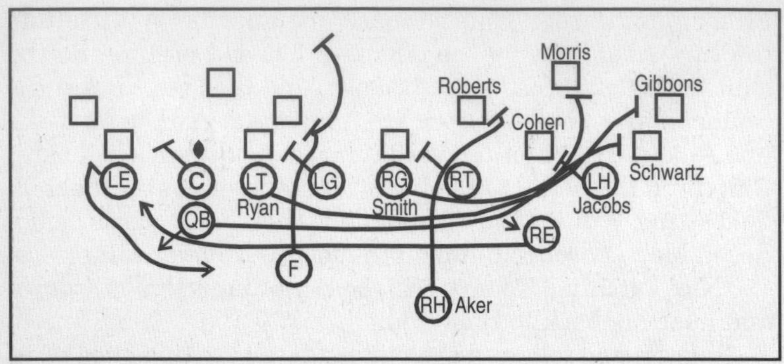

"The number-one block is against the tackle, Cohen!" Ralston quickly wrote Cohen's name above the defensive left tackle.

"That was Jacobs's responsibility," he said, writing Jacobs's name on the card. Ralston wrote Schwartz's name below the defensive left-end position. "Smith did a good job on Schwartz for the second tackle. The third one was a delayed block by Ryan on Gibbons. Ryan's timing and block were perfect."

Ralston paused and glanced at Aker before continuing. "Now," he said, "we come to the fourth block—the block that ensures a gain, or, as we have just seen, creates a loss. It's the block against the inside linebacker. In this instance, against Roberts." He wrote Roberts's name above the position shown on the card.

When he continued, the coach's voice was hard and precise. "You never touched Cohen, Jacobs. And, as a consequence, he had a clean shot at Whittemore."

"He sure did," Whittemore murmured ruefully, shaking his head.

Jacobs's face flushed and he shook his head. "I got mixed up," he said sheepishly. "I went for Roberts—"

"Roberts is Aker's man," Ralston said softly, "and he helped Cohen make the tackle. Neither of you—*neither* you, *nor* Aker—blocked Roberts out of the play."

Ralston turned to the other half of the touchdown-twin combination. "And you, Aker?"

Travis Aker shrugged. "I missed him, Coach."

There was a long silence. Ralston's eyes remained fixed on Aker's face. "All right," Ralston said at last. "We'll run the same play. This time, stay focused and go for the right man, and . . . *let's do it right!*"

Ralston handed the play card to Nik Nelson and stepped back out of the huddle. "All right, Hilton," he said quietly. "Let's go."

Soapy eyed Chip and winked significantly. Chip nodded. He knew what the redhead was thinking. Coach Ralston had known all along what was going on in the huddle. Coach knew what was up!

"On three," Chip said. "Ready, break!" The team broke out of the huddle and fell into position on the line of scrimmage.

Chip took the ball on the count of three and faked just as he had on the previous play. After handing the ball to Montague, he again headed for Speed. Just as before, Speed backed away from the block. Chip slowed down and turned to see Biggie and Junior Roberts again pulling Whitty to his feet. Jacobs and Aker were sprawled on the ground at the line of scrimmage. Chip started back to the huddle, but the blast of Ralston's whistle brought him to a halt.

"That's it," the head coach said sourly. "Three laps and go in."

There was a brief, uncertain pause before the players started their laps. Chip, Soapy, and Speed took off around the field together without a word. When they made the first turn, Chip broke the silence. "Coach knew it all the time, guys."

"You mean the trouble in the huddle?" Speed asked, turning his head to cast a questioning look at Chip.

"Right!" Chip nodded.

"He sure did, Chip!" Soapy grinned. "I'm glad you kept your head. I would have told off those two troublemakers the first time they opened their mouths."

"It wasn't easy," Chip admitted.

The three pals matched long strides and continued on around the field. Behind them, Biggie, Red, Whitty, and Fireball dug along in dogged pursuit. Chip, Speed, and Soapy sprinted the last fifty yards and then slowed down to a jog as they finished the last lap and passed in front of Coach Ralston and his assistants.

Nik Nelson elbowed Sullivan and jerked a thumb toward the other end of the field. "The huddle lawyers are at it again!" he said sarcastically.

Lagging far behind the rest of the squad, Travis Aker and Jack Jacobs jogged leisurely along, laughing. In front of the bleachers they slowed down to a walk. Ralston turned at that instant and saw the two players. He muttered something and blasted his whistle. Aker and Jacobs cast startled glances at the grim coach and then broke into a trot.

Ralston waited until they reached him and then gestured toward the field. "Three *more* laps!" he said sharply. "And I mean *running* laps!"

The two sophomores continued around the field while the staff of coaches grimly watched. When the two players finished their third lap, the coaches walked slowly toward their cabin.

"That might help," Nelson said succinctly.

"It's a start," Ralston said shortly.

"They don't know the plays," Rockwell said softly.

"Then we'll teach them the plays," Ralston said quickly. "And," he continued grimly, "we'll make them or break them, this week!"

CHAPTER 7

Cunning Duplicity

CHIP HILTON looked upfield to the thirty-five-yard line where the ball rested on the kicking tee. The Wesleyan front-line players were spaced along the thirty-five-yard line waiting for the referee's whistle to start the scrimmage. Chip's State University teammates, garbed in their traditional red and blue school colors, were moving restlessly about in their receiving positions.

Without even looking toward the sideline, Chip knew that Speed, Biggie, Joe Maxim, Ace Gibbons, and Mike Brennan were grouped in front of the State University bench. He could hear their yells of encouragement and he knew they were sincere, but he also knew how they felt. He knew how tough it was for a starter to watch and encourage the team from the sidelines.

He took a long breath and moved back to the goal line. From that spot he could see Jack Jacobs standing on his left, five yards from the sideline, and, directly opposite, Travis Aker on the right sideline. The coaches had given the two newcomers a lot of attention the past two days. Chip couldn't help thinking that maybe that was all they really needed—attention and understanding.

His heart was pounding and his legs felt as if they were made of straw as an official came trotting down the field and took a position on the goal line. Then the referee blasted his whistle. The Wesleyan kicker started slowly forward, and the ball was in the air before Chip heard the *thump* of shoe against pigskin. With that magical sound, his tension vanished.

The ball shot out and up and straight down the middle of the field, straight toward Chip on a high end-over-end arc. He gathered in the ball just inside the ten-yard line and followed Fireball's broad back up the middle of the field toward the apex of the wedge his teammates had formed. Chip was hit on the thirty but made it to the thirty-five before he was downed.

There wasn't a sound in the huddle as Chip called for a shift to the right with himself carrying the ball over right tackle on a keeper play. "Seventeen on three!" he said sharply. "Let's go!"

On the snap count of three, Chip took the ball from Leopoulos, pivoted to the right, and faked to Fireball. The big fullback's arms were crossed in front of his chest, and Chip held the ball on his right hip as he faked with his left hand. Then he continued along the line, prepared for the fake to Aker. But Aker slipped, and Chip ran head-on into the arms of the surprised, unblocked Wesleyan linebacker.

The referee's whistle stopped the play at the line of scrimmage, but that didn't stop the tackler. He carried Chip back five yards and dumped him unceremoniously on the thirty-yard line. Chip was shaken up on the play, but he scrambled quickly to his feet and hurried into the huddle as the official had a few words with the overexcited Wesleyan player.

"My fault, Hilton," Travis Aker said ruefully. "I slipped."

"Forget it," Chip said quietly. "Same formation! Buttonhook pass to Aker! On two. Break!"

The play was a takeoff on the keeper. Once again, Chip faked to Fireball and continued on for the fake to Aker. This time, Aker's timing was perfect! Chip made the fake, drifted back, faked a pass toward the right sideline, and then hit Aker on the State forty-five-yard line just as he buttonhooked back. Aker pivoted and made it to the midfield stripe before he was downed.

"*That*," Fireball declared happily when he reached the huddle, "was a pass!"

"Nice catch. Formation left," Chip said calmly. "Twenty-four on two! That's you, Fireball! Draw play! Straight-away! Break!"

Chip took the ball on the "two" count, pivoted to the left, and slipped the ball under Fireball's arms. Then he continued on out along the line, faked to Jacobs, and faded back as if to pass. When he looked back, Fireball was down on the Wesleyan thirty-eight-yard line for a twelve-yard gain!

Chip could almost feel the confident exultation emanating from his teammates. This was the first varsity experience for seven of the players on the offensive squad. Only Soapy, Whitty, and Fireball had played varsity ball besides himself. Aker and Jacobs had seemingly blended in with the rest of the newcomers, and there wasn't a sound when he called the play.

"Formation left! Thirty-eight on one! That's you, Jacobs. Break!"

Hilton faked to Fireball, slipped the ball to Jacobs, and once more faded back to fake the pass. The sophomore halfback went into the line at full speed but was hit hard after a two-yard gain. Jacobs got slowly to his feet, casting a surly glance at Ryan and Whittemore as he took his place in the huddle, but he didn't say anything.

"Same shift," Chip said confidently. "Pass play 190. Montague across! Break!"

Chip faked to Fireball and then continued out to the left for the fake to Jacobs. From his position five yards behind the line, Jacobs should have screened into the line at the precise moment Chip arrived for the fake, but he was too slow, just as Aker had been earlier. Chip arrived too soon for Jacobs's slow screen, and the Wesleyan right end, tackle, and linebacker found it unnecessary to concentrate on Jacobs and a possible thrust through the line.

Instead, they rushed Chip and chased him back for a ten-yard loss. Chip had to eat the ball and ended up sprawled flat on his back on the Wesleyan forty-six-yard line. A ten-yard loss! He got slowly to his feet and walked thoughtfully back to the huddle.

"I was wide open," Montague said uncertainly.

"I know, Monty," Chip said. "I couldn't get the ball away."

"What happened?" Fireball asked.

"Nothing," Chip said quietly. "All right. Same shift. Buttonhook to Jacobs. On the two count."

The pass called for the same fakes and ballhandling as in the previous play. This time, everything clicked. Fireball faked beautifully as he cut ahead of Chip, and Jacobs screened Chip with perfect timing at the line of scrimmage. Chip faded back and hit Jacobs on the Wesleyan thirty-yard line just as the left halfback buttonhooked back.

Jacobs circled and, picking up a block from Whittemore, headed for the goal line. But just when it looked as if the speeding receiver might go all the way, he foolishly turned to look back. The turn broke his stride just enough to enable the Wesleyan safety man to make a desperate dive tackle. His outstretched hands latched onto Jacobs's arm.

The ball squirted out! *Fumble!*

Churning bodies piled up in a wild scramble for the ball. The umpire dug down deeply into the mound of players and then patted a Wesleyan jersey. It was Wesleyan's ball, first and ten, on their own twelve-yard line. Ralston sent in his defensive squad for the first time. Despite the fumble, the

State fans gave Chip and his teammates a big hand as they trotted off the field.

Chip took off his helmet and dropped down on the bench between Soapy and Fireball. Something about the touchdown twins' playing was beginning to come into focus.

"Tough break! We'll get it back," Fireball said shortly.

"Yeah," Soapy agreed. He elbowed Chip. "By the way, Chipper, what went wrong with the seventeen play and the 190 pass?"

"Bad timing."

Soapy's eyes shot toward Aker and Jacobs, who were standing on the sideline. "Yeah," the redhead said, nodding his head vigorously, "wasn't it though?"

There was plenty of room on the bench, but the touchdown twins remained standing, holding their helmets and turning from time to time to scan the bleachers. "They must be waiting for someone to ask them for their autographs," Soapy growled.

"Autographs!" Fireball repeated. "Those two wannabes will be has-beens before they've *ever been!*"

"They've always spoken well of you," Chip said lightly.

Fireball grunted. "Yeah right! They've never spoken well of *anybody,* except themselves."

Wesleyan put the ball into play then and conversation ceased. The visitors were lined up for their first offensive series and tried the most often used play in football, the off-tackle smash.

The Wesleyan left halfback took the handoff from his quarterback and angled for the hole. But he didn't get far. Biggie Cohen and Mike Brennan brushed the blockers aside as if they were mosquitoes and smashed the runner to the ground for no gain.

Next the Wesleyan quarterback tried a pass out into the flat, which Ace Gibbons knocked down, then a spread play that gained two yards. On fourth down, the kicking unit came in from the sidelines. Speed Morris and Gary Young trotted back to the center of the field and waited for the kick.

Standing on his own four-yard line, the Wesleyan kicker barely got the ball away. But it was a good kick, a high, lazy floater that went spinning far above Young's head. Gary took a quick look at the charging ends and the rest of the converging players and extended his arm above his head, waving his hand from side to side, signaling for a fair catch.

Speed backed him up, shouting words of encouragement. Chip glanced up at the wobbly ball and then concentrated on Young. The little sophomore was watching the descending pigskin as if hypnotized, swaying slightly as he concentrated on the ball.

"He's going to drop it," Chip said, gripping Soapy's arm.

"Speed!" Soapy yelled. "Heads up!"

The ball took one last swerve and shot over Young's head. Gary moved back, but he was off balance and couldn't hang on to the ball. It went spinning and bounding away toward the coffin corner, with Speed in swift pursuit and the Wesleyan players hard on the speedster's heels.

It looked as if the ball might go out of bounds on the ten-yard line, but the Wesleyan players were so close that Speed decided not to take a chance. He dove headlong and curled his body safely around the elusive ball on State's seven-yard line. Ralston had Chip and the offensive team on its way almost as soon as the referee's whistle killed the play.

Keyed up by the unexpected break, the Wesleyan defensive unit was determined to keep State pinned back against the goal. When State came out of the huddle, the visitors deployed quickly into a 4-4-3 defense. Chip had called for a draw play, with Fireball carrying up the middle. Now he was tempted to use a check signal and change to a pass play, but he let it go and Fireball barely made a yard.

Second down, nine yards to go.

Back in the huddle, Chip studied the visitors' defensive captain. "They're set for a running play," he muttered, half to himself and half to his teammates. "Just what we want. Heads up, now. Straight formation. Ninety-one X pass on the fake draw. Count of one. Whitty and Monty up the sidelines. Heads up. The pass will be to the outside. Let's go!"

He took the ball from Leopoulos on the count of one, faked to Fireball, and dropped back in the pocket for the pass. Whittemore and Montague drove straight upfield for five yards and then out and up the sidelines. Fireball buttonhooked behind the Wesleyan guard, and Aker and Jacobs formed the pass-protection pocket with Soapy and O'Malley.

Ordinarily the pocket gave Chip plenty of time to get set for a pass. Soapy and O'Malley did a good job this time too. But the Wesleyan ends drove through and over Aker and Jacobs as if they weren't there. Chip was concentrating on the receivers, but the touchdown twins' weak blocking efforts were obvious.

They dove under the charging ends, rolling ineffectively along the ground. Chip had no time to pass. He barely had time to cover the ball with his arms before he was snowed under by the rush of the big wing men and dropped savagely on the State two-yard line.

Third down, fifteen yards to go.

The big ends had dumped Chip hard, but it wasn't the force of the tackle that stunned him. No, it was the sudden realization that Aker and Jacobs were outsmarting him. They were cleverly camouflaging their intention to sabotage every play in which they did not carry the ball or catch a pass. And they meant to make him look bad in the process!

On the way to his position in the huddle, he thought it through. During the past two days the touchdown twins had completely reversed their attitudes. They had kept quiet in the huddle, mastered the plays, and carried out their assignments to the letter. Aker and Jacobs had fooled the coaches! And, Chip reflected ruefully, they had fooled him too.

With the ball resting on the State two-yard line, Chip's teammates had formed the huddle deep in the end zone.

There had been some talking while they assembled, but all conversation ceased when he took his position. Chip was bitterly angry now. Football was a team game. Even competitors in individual sports such as cross country, tennis, and golf understood the importance of team effort. But these two players wanted to play on their own and at the expense of everybody else. One thing was for sure: he had completely fallen for the cunning duplicity of the touchdown twins!

CHAPTER 8

A Gale of Laughter

CHIP HILTON didn't know what to do. Right then, he was gripped by a feeling of frustrated anger. Worrying about the opponents and the plays was enough to keep any field general occupied. When a quarterback also had to worry about his halfback teammates pulling fake blocks, it was *too* much!

There was time for one more play before the end of the half, and Chip didn't know whether he should risk the danger of a safety or kick. *You've got to kick,* he told himself. He looked up to meet the determined faces of Fireball and Soapy. And just like that, he changed his mind. He thought through his options and chose the most daring play on the list.

"That's it!" Chip breathed to himself. *Aker and Jacobs can't possibly mess it up. They're not even near the ball.*

Chip knew he could count on Fireball and Soapy. The play he had in mind called for a good fake by the burly fullback, and much depended on a good block by Soapy. He glanced straight at Aker and then eyed Jacobs. "All right," he said grimly, "let's have some blocking from you guys this time. Formation right! Eighteen with a keeper! Four count! Let's go!"

When he was in position behind Leopoulos, Chip started his count and took the snap on four. Then he faked with his left hand and held the ball on his right hip with his right hand. Fireball faked beautifully, thrusting his crossed arms over Chip's hand as if it were the ball. He then drove into the line as if his life depended on a five-yard gain.

"Now for it," Chip breathed. He forced himself to pivot slowly to the right, transferring the ball at the same time from his right to his left hand. He held the ball on his left hip, out of sight of the visitors' charging linemen. He saw Soapy pull out of the line and start to the left as Whittemore pinned the visitors' big right tackle.

Soapy cut just outside the Wesleyan tackle, who was blocked by Whittemore, and Chip continued on, trotting leisurely. When he reached the scrimmage line, Soapy cut swiftly across in front of Chip and headed upfield. Chip then discarded all pretense, pulled the ball up under his arm, and followed Soapy at full speed.

"Bootleg play!" the Wesleyan safety man yelled, dashing toward Chip. "Watch the quarterback!"

Soapy dropped the right linebacker, and Chip sped toward the center of the field. It was the right move, because Montague had cut across from his position on the right side of the State formation and was charging at full speed for the Wesleyan safety.

Chip slowed his pace enough to let Montague get in the lead and then reversed his field as the tall end timed his block and cut the safety's feet from under him.

Chip could see daylight ahead of him now. He was on his way! He stretched his long legs and headed for the Wesleyan goal line, sixty long yards ahead. Behind him, Chip could hear pounding feet, but he didn't look back!

He concentrated on a straight line to the opposite end of the field. As he passed the midfield stripe, he heard a tremendous shout from the stands. That told him one of the visitors was closing the gap or close enough to make a try for him. Chip called upon all his speed.

He never saw the Wesleyan player dive for him, but he sensed that the danger was past when he flashed across the Wesleyan forty. The crowd noise died down as he cut across the thirty, the twenty, and the ten. But it picked up again when he crossed the goal line for the first score of the game.

He handed the ball to the official and breathed a deep sigh. The half was over. All he had to do now was kick for the extra point or elect to try a two-point running or passing play. Then his teammates joyously ganged up on him, smacking him on the back and punching him good-naturedly.

Chip was still breathing hard, but he felt as though a great weight had lifted from his chest. The strategy had paid off, and he felt sure Aker and Jacobs now realized that he was aware of their trickery. The incident in the huddle must have brought that home to them. Now he could fight fire with fire.

The referee's whistle sounded as State lined up for the extra-point kick. "Fireball, you hold the ball," he said softly. He paused for a moment and then looked straight at Aker. "Block their left end this time, Aker."

Chip's and Aker's eyes locked. Then Aker shifted his glance, and Chip turned his attention to the other member of the touchdown combination. "The right end is your man, Jacobs," he said pointedly. "Stay on your feet."

Not a player moved. Chip waited a second longer. "All right, Leopoulos," he said, "snap the ball on the count of two! Let's go!"

Wesleyan was lined up on the other side of the ball, and as soon as his teammates were in position, Chip mentally drew an imaginary line between Fireball's holding position and the center of the uprights.

The ball came back on the "two" count, and Fireball plunked it down on the line. But it was the first time the big fullback had held the ball for an extra-point kick, and his fingers slipped off the ball just as the toe of Chip's kicking shoe crashed through.

Chip got the ball up in the air, but it was wide of the mark. The score at the half: State 6, Wesleyan 0.

Coach Ralston devoted the entire intermission to the offense. He was obviously disturbed by State's inability to move the ball. When time was up, he called on Chip to handle the kickoff duties.

Chip placed the ball on the kicking tee and glanced along the thirty-five-yard line at Biggie, Speed, Red, Eddie Anderson, Mike Brennan, Ace Gibbons, and Joe Maxim. Only Soapy, Fireball, and Whitty were missing from last year's championship team.

Chip signaled he was ready, and the referee blasted his whistle. Starting slowly forward, Chip's teammates matched his last few strides as he booted the ball into the air. The wave of players headed downfield after the ball in choreographed unison. The kick was high and carried to the five-yard line. Chip, playing the traditional role of the kicker—the last tackler—followed slowly behind the wave of State tacklers.

Up ahead, Biggie Cohen and Ace Gibbons raced side by side through the Wesleyan blockers and dropped the ball carrier so hard on the fifteen-yard line that he fumbled. But Wesleyan recovered and it was their ball, first and ten, on their own twelve-yard line.

Coach Ralston sent in the substitutes when the referee's whistle killed the ball. As soon as the fans saw Chip give his replacement a pat on the back and start for the State bench, they gave him a round of applause.

Ralston met Chip at the sideline and grasped his arm. "You pulled us out of a bad hole in the first half, Chip. Nice going!"

"I had a lot of help, Coach," Chip said quickly.

"I know," Ralston agreed blandly. "By the way, weren't you having trouble in the huddle? Some unnecessary talking?"

"No, Coach. Not a bit."

"Everyone know the plays?"

"Yes, sir."

"Well, then, how about the blocking?"

"It could be better, Coach," Chip admitted.

Ralston nodded grimly. "I know."

A roar from the stands drew Curly Ralston's and Chip's attention back to the field just in time for them to see the ball sail over the Wesleyan receiver's head and into the arms of Speed Morris, who was quickly brought down on State's forty-yard line. The visitors had hoped to surprise State's defensive secondary but were instead surprised by Speed's interception.

"Back you go," Ralston said, releasing Chip's arm. "Offense, let's put some points on the board."

Chip joined his teammates in the huddle.

"Hey, the defense got this ball, and we want to play with it awhile," Ace Gibbons said, grinning.

"Sorry, Ace, the coach wants some points on the board," Chip retorted.

"Oh, no," Speed moaned. "Can't we run the ball just once?"

"Nice grab, Speed, but it's Coach's orders," Chip said as State's defensive team jogged to the sidelines.

"Heads up, now! Straight handoff to Aker. Ball on three."

They broke out of the huddle, and Bebop Leopoulos stood poised over the ball until his teammates were set. Chip had moved behind Bebop and turned to judge the distance to their own goal. He checked the positions of his teammates and started the count. "Hut one, hut two, hut three!"

Not a Wesleyan player broke through the State line. And Bebop's snap was, as always, on the mark for the quarterback. Travis stumbled forward, gaining slightly more than a yard. That's the way the series went, forcing State to bring in the punting crew on fourth down and a long four yards for a first down.

The teamwork between the snapper and kicker was smooth and flawless. Bebop's long snap came directly back into Chip's outstretched hands, just over his kicking foot. Not a motion was wasted as Chip took his stride and slanted a low, powerful spinner toward the sideline. The ball took off as straight as a ruler's edge and sailed out of bounds on the Wesleyan five-yard line.

The referee's whistle killed the ball as the new units for each team came onto the field. Again, Chip drew cheers from the stands as he ran off the field. The Wesleyan quarterback tried a running play that was smeared at the line of scrimmage. He then tried his passing game, but to no avail. Their second and third downs were wasted on incomplete passes that fell short of the intended receivers.

Once again, the visitors' punter responded with a superb effort, sending a high, wobbly punt almost to the State forty-five-yard line. The Wesleyan ends were right on top of Speed when he called for the fair catch. As soon as Speed caught the ball, Ralston waved his arm and Chip and the rest of the offense dashed onto the field.

Chip's thoughts raced ahead, and when he faced his teammates in the huddle, he had his campaign all mapped out. State had run roughshod over Wesleyan the previous season to win 40-14, and it was obvious to every State player on the field that the visitors remembered the beating. They were playing as hard and as desperately as if it were a regularly scheduled game, as if victory meant the conference championship. Chip wanted another touchdown. Quickly! Six points wasn't much of a lead. He glanced at the visitors' defensive huddle. They had been showing a 4-4-3 defense. Maybe he could tighten it up a bit more.

"All right, formation left! Play 24! Cross buck by Finley! On two!"

Fireball came through with a four-yard gain, putting State directly at midfield, second down and six. Chip flipped a short over-the-line pass to Montague for a gain of five yards to make it third down with a yard to go and then called on Fireball again. The big man's carry was good for three yards and the first down.

With the ball resting on the State forty-two yard line, he went deep into his repertory of plays and came up with a takeoff on the keeper he had used on his touchdown run. "Formation right!" he said sharply. "Pass play 96! Fake boot leg option! On the count of one! Let's make it a good one."

Leopoulos snapped the ball on the "one." Chip faked to Fireball and then pivoted around and hid the ball on his hip as he had done on the touchdown sprint. This time, however, the Wesleyan right end wasn't taking chances; he concentrated on Chip and was easy pickings for Soapy. The redhead pulled out of the line and, instead of cutting upfield, drove hard for the big end, cutting him down expertly.

As soon as Soapy blocked the end, Chip faded back and looked for his pass receivers. Jacobs and Aker were running down the right side of the field and Montague had cut across behind the line of scrimmage. Whittemore had thrown a fake block at the Wesleyan right tackle and then continued down the middle of the field. Just as Chip dug his right foot in the ground and poised to make the throw, Whittemore cut abruptly to the left and raced along the sideline.

Chip gauged the distance between Whittemore and the Wesleyan safety and let the ball fly. He breathed a sigh of relief when he saw that Whitty's long legs were pulling him away from his opponent.

"It's going to be close," Chip muttered.

But it wasn't close. Whittemore was six inches taller than the defender and, without breaking stride, reached above the safety's outstretched hands and easily pulled in the ball. He kept right on going up the sideline, swiftly outdistancing the Wesleyan player. Whitty went all the way for the touchdown. Seconds later, Coach Ralston nudged Speed, who raced in to report for Fireball as Chip dropped back to try for the extra point.

The ball came twirling back, and the rest was automatic and seemingly routine. The two lifelong friends and teammates had executed these synchronized movements countless times in the Hilton backyard and at Valley Falls High School. Speed plunked the ball down in perfect position, and Chip caught it just right. The ball went flying end over end between the uprights to make the score State 13, Wesleyan 0.

Ralston sent in the kickoff unit right after the referee raised his arms over his head. And, once again, Chip kicked off. This time, he gave the kick a little extra power. The ball landed in the visitors' end zone, bounding and rolling out of bounds. Wesleyan had time for one more play, a desperation pass Speed knocked down to end the game.

Chip had been sitting quietly on the bench beside Soapy. When the game ended, they trudged wearily through the crowd of spectators flowing down out of the bleachers and onto the field. Travis Aker and Jack Jacobs followed slowly behind them, unnoticed by the two friends. Someone tapped Chip on the arm, and he looked over to see Skip Miller. Skip was wearing a State University sweater and had a backpack over one shoulder. He smiled widely and extended his hand. "Nice going, Chip," the high school star said. "You were great!"

Chip smiled, murmured something, and then turned and nodded toward Soapy. "Skip, this is my friend, Soapy Smith. Soapy, this is Skip Miller." Soapy had been staring in openmouthed amazement at Skip.

"Wow! It can't be," he said weakly, his eyebrows arching in surprise. "Incredible! Am I seeing double?" He shook his head and gulped as he sized up the tall youngster. Then he extended his hand and shook his head again. "If I didn't know better, I'd think you were Chip's little brother."

"Oh, I forgot!" Skip added. He pulled a sports magazine out of his backpack and thrust it into Chip's hands. "Take a look! It just hit the stands! Look at the cover!"

Chip gazed in surprise at the full-page headshot of a State University player. "Why, that's—"

Chip was startled by a forced gale of laughter directly behind him. "That's right!" Travis Aker managed. "It's Chip Hilton!"

"Yeah," Jack Jacobs added. "Must be a new comic book!"

CHAPTER 9

We Choose Our Friends

SKIP MILLER turned in shocked surprise to face Travis Aker and Jack Jacobs. "What do you mean?" he demanded.

Aker pointed to the magazine. "The comic," he said. "You know, the all-American quarterback." He paused and hooked his thumb over his shoulder toward Chip. "State's gift to football."

Skip's face was a picture of puzzled surprise. "You're kidding, right?"

Aker's face dropped its sneer, and he glanced from Skip to Chip and back again to the tall high school star. "Hey," he sneered, "what's your name? Hilton?"

Skip shook his head. "No, my name is Miller."

"Good thing for you," Aker said. "It's bad enough you have to look like him."

"You're sure your name isn't Hilton?" Jacobs persisted.

"I'm sure," Skip nodded, frowning. "What's going on?"

"Don't pay any attention to them, Skip. They're great kidders," Soapy said sourly. "Especially when it comes to football. They *think* they're football players."

"I don't understand," Skip said uncertainly. "Aren't you guys on the same team?"

"Oh, we're on the same team all right," Jacobs said sarcastically. "But you would never know it."

"That's right," Aker added. "The great man, the great Hilton, only knows two kinds of plays. His own and those of his friends. He passes everyone else up."

"When did I pass you up?" Chip asked calmly.

"Lots of times," Jacobs retorted angrily.

"If you want to be specific," Aker added, "on that last pass play."

"And on every play since you got dumped on the goal line," Jacobs accused.

Soapy moved over in front of the touchdown twins. "He got dumped because you guys didn't do any blocking," he said sharply.

"They faked the blocks, Soapy," Chip explained. He nodded at Aker and continued. "I'll admit you guys surprised me with your clumsy imitations, but that didn't have anything to do with the last pass. You were both covered. Whitty wasn't."

"Naturally," Jacobs drawled. "Say, haven't you been reading the papers, Travis?"

"No. Why?"

"Then you don't know about State's all-American passing combination, the great Hilton and Whittemore?"

"Well, I haven't been doing much reading," Aker said pointedly, "but I happen to know that Hilton and Whittemore work together at Grayson's."

"What's that got to do with anything?" Chip demanded.

"Just buddy-buddy," Aker said. "You know, buddy-buddy, palsy-walsy. On the field and off the field."

Chip smiled and nodded agreement. "You're right, Aker," he said coolly. "Coach chooses the team, but we can choose our friends. See you later."

"Don't worry about us. We'll be around, Hilton," Jacobs said darkly.

"And don't you two forget to bring your newspaper clippings for the next scrimmage," Soapy said. "Nobody knew who you were out there today."

Aker and Jacobs turned away, glowering and muttering.

Chip, Soapy, and Skip continued on their way.

Skip whistled softly in relief. "Nice guys," he said thoughtfully. "Real nice guys. I'm glad they're not on *my* team."

"Team!" Soapy echoed. "Humph! They don't know what the word means."

"I know," Skip said, nodding. "I saw what happened."

"I hope Coach Ralston saw it," Soapy said grouchily.

"Don't worry about that," Chip replied. "Coach Ralston doesn't miss much."

"Look, I've got to be going home," Skip said, patting his backpack. "Summer reading for my literature class! Sure glad to have met you, Soapy. Oh, and Chip, please don't forget about the job."

"I won't, Skip."

As Skip walked swiftly away, Chip and Soapy studied the front page of the magazine. The picture was a color headshot of Chip wearing a red and blue helmet with the familiar white stripe running over the top and down the front.

The headline read:

STATE'S ALL-AMERICAN QUARTERBACK ON THE SPOT

"What's that all about?" Soapy asked curiously, reaching for the magazine. He leafed through the pages until he found another picture of Chip. It was an action shot and showed his pal passing in the A & M game.

Soapy jabbed a finger into the page. "Now *that's* football!" He scanned the pages as they walked slowly down the path toward their cabin at Camp Sundown.

Reading the magazine, Soapy lagged behind as Chip walked on ahead. He opened the door, and his friends met him with a chorus of good-natured gibes and jeers.

"Chip Hilton's on the spot!" Whitty cried.

"What big feet you have, Red Riding Hood," Red chortled.

"They'll be pointing at the triple-threat star," Fireball chirped.

Speed shook a magazine in the air. "It says here that the David Copperfield of the gridiron is so clever at concealing the ball that he often forgets where he hides it. How about that?"

Chip made a grab for the magazine. "Come on, Speed—"

"There's more of them," Speed protested kindly. "Bill Bell brought out a whole box full and handed them out to everyone."

"He would," Chip groaned.

The kidding lasted while Chip and the guys were showering, but it ended when they reached the dining room in Camp Sundown's main building. Ralston called for a strategy session right after dinner, and two hours later when the meeting broke up, the Statesmen were too tired to think of anything except heading for their bunks.

Sunday passed pleasantly for Chip and his friends, beginning with morning services. Coach Rockwell had arranged for a van to take players to church in the nearby town of Antlers. The State University players genuinely appreciated how welcome everyone made them feel in the warm, peaceful surroundings. Right at home and singing in his best off-key voice, Soapy joyously joined in the familiar hymns.

Back at Camp Sundown, the team spent the rest of the day reading and relaxing from the rigors of collegiate football. Monday, right after breakfast, the squad was assembled for a brief meeting.

"This is the last week of our time here at Sundown," Ralston said softly. "As you know, we play Mercer in a breakup game on Saturday. Right after the game, you are free to leave with your parents or friends. A bus will take the rest of you to University.

"Classes start on the following Monday, so this is an important week in our football plans. I promise you a week of action."

The action started as soon as they reported to the practice field, and it continued through the day and into the evening. It was the same all day Tuesday. Wednesday afternoon, following the warm-up drill, Coach Ralston waved them to the empty bleachers.

"This scrimmage is going to be different," the tall coach said evenly. "It's almost time we separated the men from the boys, and we're going to get a look at some of you on both offense and defense. We'll start out with the Red Team kicking off. Blue squad, get set to receive. Let's go!"

"This is it," Chip breathed. "Now I'll really find out if Aker and Jacobs are going to play ball."

He placed the ball in his favorite position on the kicking tee and backed up to the thirty-yard line. He glanced from left to right and back again along the thirty-five-yard line where his Red Team was standing in readiness. Whitty, Ryan, O'Malley, Leopoulos, and Jacobs were on the left side of the ball and Soapy, Logan, Montague, Aker, and Fireball were on the right.

Ralston blasted the whistle. Chip started slowly forward, picked up the wave of blockers, and plunked his toe into the ball. The pigskin flew end over end down to the five-yard line and into the eager arms of Ace Gibbons. The big halfback raced up the middle of the field behind the wedge. Most of Chip's teammates had been dumped unceremoniously before they got anywhere near the ball carrier, but Fireball and Soapy broke up the wedge. Chip knifed through for the tackle.

That first big gain was only the beginning. For this scrimmage, Ralston had inserted Chip into the third line of defense, but he was making half the tackles himself. Aker and Jacobs were blocked out of every play, and the inexperienced Red Team just couldn't stand up against the hard-driving blocks of the Blue Team.

Blue Team scored in seven plays. Then, to add insult to injury, Gibbons kicked a perfect point after to put his squad out in front, 7-0, after little more than four minutes of play.

Chip chose to receive, and big Mike Brennan booted the ball straight to him on the goal line. Chip darted forward and glanced up ahead at Ryan, O'Malley, Leopoulos, Soapy, and Logan. The five linemen were supposed to drop back from the restraining line to help with the wedge, but they weren't fast enough. Biggie, Maxim, Schwartz, Brennan, and Roberts bore down on him like a runaway truck barreling down a mountain. Chip didn't have a chance; he was mobbed on the twelve-yard line and buried under a pile of tacklers. These were State University teammates, but in this intrasquad scrimmage, no quarter was asked or given.

He tried Fireball up the middle on a draw play and the big fullback barely made two yards. On a keeper from formation right, Aker was slow coming up to the line, and Cohen, Bob Horton, and Brennan charged through Montague and Logan and met Chip before he could reach the line of scrimmage. On third down, Chip called an end-around play, from Montague to Whitty. The big end was thrown for a three-yard loss. Aker dove into the line and fell to his knees. Jacobs made a try for Cohen and slipped under the big tackle's hands without even making contact.

Chip was sick at heart. This was really happening! The touchdown twins knew the plays, but they weren't going to help anyone except themselves.

On fourth down Chip called for a punt formation. And, just as it had been in the Wesleyan game, Aker and Jacobs failed to block the charging ends. Horton and Red were on top of him, hands stretched high, when he booted the ball. He barely got the kick away.

Robert "Speed" Morris took the ball at midfield and raced all the way to the Red Team's thirty, where Chip and

Fireball teamed up to make the tackle. On the next play, Blue Team quarterback Gary Young passed over Aker's head to Schwartz, and Red scored standing up. Ace Gibbons knocked down another perfect placement, and the Blue Team led, 14-0.

Chip turned back upfield, his eyes blazing and with anger in his heart. Soapy, Fireball, Whitty, and Leopoulos trudged silently beside him. Chip didn't even see Coach Ralston. He nearly walked into him. The head coach was standing on the fifty-yard line, smack in the center of the field.

"Hold it right here, men," Curly Ralston said, windmilling his arms to the rest of the players. "I want to make a few changes with the two squads on the field for a few series."

The players on the sideline and the two units on the field ran up and surrounded the tall coach. "There ought to be some way to make the plays go," Ralston said evenly. "Suppose we try a few substitutions: Brennan for Leopoulos, Cohen for Ryan, Maxim for Logan, Morris for Jacobs, and Gibbons for Aker. That's it for now! On the double!"

Chip sprinted for his receiving position in front of the goal. This was more like it!

Leopoulos, now on the Blue Team, booted the ball, and Finley, standing on the twenty-yard line directly in front of Chip, took it at a dead run. The speedy fullback was brought down on the forty-yard line before he hustled back into the huddle. "Excellent! Excellent!" he said jubilantly.

"That's right, baby!" Soapy added, his face wreathed in smiles while a bead of sweat perched on his red nose. "We'll kill 'em!"

Chip called formation right and the end-around reverse. He took Mike Brennan's pass from center on the count of two, faked to Fireball and then Ace, slipped the ball to Monty, and headed out for his block. As Chip rounded right tackle, he saw Whitty take the ball from Monty and race toward him. Up ahead, Jacobs saw Chip coming and advanced warily.

Timing his block, Chip faked with his head to bring Jacobs's hands up and then ducked under them for a cross-body block. Jacobs had reached out with his hands to fend off the block, but once Chip committed himself to his move, Jacobs made no further effort to use his hands. Instead, he took a short step forward and brought his knee up in a vicious kick that landed flush on Chip's jaw.

Chip never finished the block; he fell heavily to the ground. On the verge of a blackout, he was still intent on completing the block. Instinct brought him scrambling to his feet, but his head was swimming and he had to drop down on one knee.

"What's the matter with you, Hilton?" Jacobs snarled. "Out of your head? The whistle killed the play. Can't you hear?"

Chip focused his eyes on Whitty and a pile of tacklers unscrambling themselves up ahead on the forty-yard line. Then he nodded uncertainly. There was no doubt about it. Jacobs was right. The whistle *had* blown.

"How'd that feel?" Jacobs continued. "How do *you* like being on the receiving end? I guess that'll hold you!"

CHAPTER 10

The Treatment

VETERAN TRAINER MURPH KELLY seemed to be weaving around in front of him, and Chip raised a hand to steady the moving figure. *Why won't he stand still?* wondered Chip. Kelly did hold still long enough to break open and thrust an ammonia capsule under his nose. The sharp, pungent scent bit through the fog, and, despite Kelly's restraining hand, Chip struggled to his feet.

"Give me a hand here, one of you," the trainer said sharply. "Help him over to the bench."

"I'm all right, Murph," Chip protested. "Just a little groggy, that's all."

"Well, *I'm* not all right!" Kelly retorted. "Out you go!"

Biggie and Soapy, their faces chiseled with worry, placed Chip's arms over their shoulders and walked him toward the sideline. Murph Kelly followed closely behind, muttering angrily.

Coach Ralston and Henry Rockwell advanced to meet them as two student trainers exchanged places with Soapy and Biggie. "All right, Chip?" Coach Rockwell asked. The student trainers handed Chip a cup of Gatorade and placed a wet towel around the back of his neck.

"Thanks, guys," Chip said, nodding to Josh and Melissa. He looked up at the two coaches. "Sure. It wasn't anything. I told Murph—"

"Chip, the quarterback is in charge of the team," Ralston said gently. "The trainer is in charge of the injuries."

Chip's face flushed. "Sorry, sir," he said, nodding. Coach Ralston turned and motioned to Toby March. "Toby, you're in on the Blue Team. Young takes Hilton's place."

Chip sat down on the bench and studied the players on the field as he gingerly worked his chin with his hand. After a few moments he shifted his glance to Jacobs and nodded grimly. Now he knew what he was up against.

He glanced toward the offensive huddle. The players were grouped around Ace Gibbons in a tight circle fifteen yards behind the ball. Gibbons was gesturing with his hands and talking rapidly. Then the referee blew his whistle to start the clock, and the teams trotted up to their positions on the line of scrimmage.

Handling the quarterbacking duties for Chip, Gary Young took the ball from Mike Brennan and pivoted left. Then he whirled around and headed toward right end. Chip saw that every player on the offensive unit was out in front of the little quarterback. *It's a keeper play, all right,* Chip thought, *but it certainly isn't one of the plays Coach gave me.*

He gazed at the scene in amazement. Then he got it. Except for Gary Young, every player on the offensive team was heading for Jacobs. And, one by one, each took a shot at him. Jacobs was hit five or six times in succession by the blockers, but none of them tried to knock him down. At the end, however, he was really clobbered and fell to the ground.

Coaches Jim Sullivan and Nik Nelson were standing a few steps away, and Chip saw the big line coach nudge

Nelson. "They're giving him the treatment," Sullivan said softly.

Nelson nodded. "It doesn't make me mad. Let's keep an eye on it though."

The defense finally brought Young down on their own three-yard line, and as soon as the referee's whistle sounded, the offensive players ran back to their huddle with more purpose. They formed quickly and then turned and dashed up to the line in formation left.

"Aker's turn," Chip whispered to himself.

He watched closely as Young pivoted to the right and then swung around to the left. And, just as before, every player on the offensive team converged on the left side of the line, headed for Aker. They got to him, too, and gave him the same treatment Jacobs had received. But it ended there. Ralston suddenly realized what was going on and rushed out on the field.

"That's enough!" Ralston bellowed angrily. "I don't go for that kind of treatment. We're a *team!* Laps! Every player on the field!"

Chip got to his feet and started around the field, but Murph Kelly stopped him. "Where do you think you're going? You come with me!"

Chip shook his head in resignation and followed the chattering trainer. As Coach Ralston had said, the trainer was in charge of the injuries.

Kelly examined Chip's jaw carefully. "It's all right," he growled, "but it seems to me that a smart quarterback like you would have enough sense to take care of himself."

"What do you mean?"

"You know what I mean! Aker and Jacobs. *Especially* Jacobs."

"He was my man on the play, Murph. It was my block."

"Sure! Sure it was! But a smart boxer never leads with his right."

"I don't get it."

Kelly grunted skeptically and eyed Chip carefully. "You understand. all right. You're not fooling me. Why couldn't you have used a straight shoulder block? Why turn sideways and leave yourself wide open? Wise up, Hilton. The so-called touchdown twins mean nothing but double trouble for you."

"I don't think so, Murph."

Kelly turned abruptly away. "Well, young man, everybody else thinks so," he said shortly. "From now on, you watch your step. Understand?"

Chip nodded and walked slowly out of the room and back up the wooded path to his cabin. He stripped and showered. The hot water felt good and helped clear his head. He was resting on his bunk when the rest of his friends arrived.

"Jaw all right?" Whitty asked.

"Sure, Whitty, I'm fine. I tried to run, but Murph wouldn't let me."

"He let us," Soapy moaned, tugging at his soaked jersey. "Some fun! Coach makes us run laps because those two guys want to play dirty football!"

"It wasn't so bad," Biggie drawled. "I'd do twenty more laps if I could see those two phonies doggin' it around the field again."

"Did you get that act they were putting on?" Red asked.

"How could you miss it!" Speed said, laughing. "Every time they passed Ralston, they hobbled as though their legs were broken."

Fireball chuckled. "And Ralston didn't even give them a second look. It was beautiful!"

"Well," Soapy concluded, "I hope Coach finally separated the men from the boys."

Soapy couldn't possibly have known it, but right then, that was exactly what Curly Ralston and his coaching staff were doing. Ralston was pacing back and forth across the living room of the cabin, and his three leading assistants,

Henry Rockwell, Nik Nelson, and Jim Sullivan, were sitting at the planning table.

Ralston finally stopped pacing and rested his hands on the edge of the table. Then he looked across at Henry Rockwell and shook his head. "It isn't going to work out, Rock."

"It's a pretty big step from the freshman team to the varsity," Rockwell said gently. "Maybe they just need a little more time."

Sullivan shifted restlessly in his chair and shook his head. "Time is right!" he said hotly. "That Jacobs ought to have about ten years for what he tried to do to Hilton this afternoon."

"Right!" Nelson added. "We lose Chip and we can kiss this year good-bye."

"I know," Ralston said thoughtfully. "Rock, s'pose you get Jacobs and Aker over here for a little chat right after dinner. Try to straighten them out."

Sullivan folded the fingers of his big right hand into a fist and rapped the table. "I'd like to straighten them out," he growled.

A brief smile flashed across Ralston's thin lips. Then he continued in even tones. "We'll go along with them a little longer, but I don't intend to get caught shorthanded on the offense or the defense. Some of the lower-ranked players will get a good look. Starting tomorrow, we'll make sure that the depth chart highlights our key players. Some of our squad may even get a look at playing both ways."

"You mean play both offense and defense?" Sullivan asked.

Ralston nodded. "Right! We've got two more days before the breakup game on Saturday. Let's see what they've got!"

Chip was sitting on the bench on the front porch of his cabin. The rattle of dishes and the jumbled voices could be heard from the dining room all the way to the cabin as his teammates enjoyed the breakup brunch. But the sounds barely registered. Chip was thinking back over the past two days of practice.

Aker and Jacobs had ignored him completely. Chip figured that was all right with him. He had learned his lesson. Never again, he vowed, would he be taken in by their trickery.

He glanced toward the field. It was only a little after eleven o'clock, but cars had been arriving steadily for the past hour. The field was nearly surrounded. Chip knew a big crowd would be there at kickoff time, packed in the bleachers.

His thoughts jumped ahead to school and his and Soapy's dormitory room in Jefferson Hall. It would be their third year in the famous old dormitory. Then he thought about his job at Grayson's and his boss, George Grayson. He was lucky to have such an understanding employer.

Feelings of nostalgia suddenly gripped Chip. The breakup game marked another milestone in his college life. There would be only one more State University training camp for him, only one more preseason stay at Camp Sundown.

His thoughts shifted to his mother back in Valley Falls. He sure wished she could be at the game today. Even as he made the wish, he knew it was impossible. Ever since his father died, she had worked for the phone company in Valley Falls. She had worked up to the position of supervisor, but from her devotion to the job, one would have thought she owned the company. Chip knew the real reason. His mother was determined to keep the family home going and to do all she could to see that he earned his college degree. Someday he would take care of the family responsibilities, but she was handling them now.

He was still buried deep in thought when he heard his teammates coming out of the dining room. A moment later Murph Kelly appeared on the steps of the camp office and bellowed for them to get going. "Hit those bunks!" the trainer yelled. "Dress at 1:30. On the field at 2:15."

When Murph Kelly roused the squad two hours later, Chip, Speed, and Fireball were already dressed in their game uniforms and waiting for the student trainers to tape their ankles. A few minutes later, Bebop Leopoulos joined them, and they trotted out on the field for their pregame kicking practice. As Chip had anticipated, the stands were jammed and cars lined every inch of the small parking area. Chip and his kicking buddies loosened up and then began their kicking.

Seconds later, a cheer erupted from the stands as the Mercer players dashed out on the field. They were wearing gold jerseys and blue pants, and they went about their warm-up work in a businesslike manner.

"Big team!" Fireball said shortly.

Before Chip could reply, Coach Ralston called them to the State bench. "We'll start with Brennan, Smith, O'Malley, Cohen, Maxim, Whittemore, and Montague on the line. Hilton, Finley, Morris, and Gibbons will be in the backfield. Brennan and Hilton, act as captains. Take the offensive unit down the field and back, Hilton."

Brennan grabbed a ball, sprinted out on the field, and plunked it down on the fifty-yard line. Chip and the rest of the team were right behind him and took their positions. "On three!" he cried. "Ready! Hut one, hut two, hut three!"

Chip felt the rhythm and the surge of power as the veterans took off on the charging signal. *This* is *more like it!*

When Chip and his teammates returned, the referee, umpire, linesman, and line judge, all garbed in striped shirts and white knickers, were waiting in the center of the field.

"All right," Ralston said, "Brennan, Hilton! Get out there for the toss. Receive if you win it. Defend the west goal if you lose."

Chip and Mike matched strides as they trotted out to the center of the field where the officials waited with two Mercer players. After the introductions, the referee turned to the Mercer captains. "Visitors' choice," he said. "Call it!"

The Mercer cocaptains chose heads, won the toss, and chose to receive. "We'll defend the west goal," Brennan said.

The referee signaled the choices to the spectators and the sidelines while Brennan and Chip shook hands with the Mercer cocaptains. Then the two Statesmen hustled back to the sideline where Ralston waited, surrounded by his players.

Chip edged into the circle between Aker and Jacobs. Then, as the inner circle of players yelled and clasped hands with Ralston in a display of team unity, Aker leaned close to Chip and ruined the moment. "Finally got your way, didn't you?" he rasped.

Chip glanced at the disgruntled halfback in surprise. "What do you mean?"

"Rockwell!" Jacobs said, elbowing him sharply in the ribs. "That's what he means. Now tell us *you* weren't responsible for getting us into trouble with him. He chewed us out all over the place."

"I wasn't," Chip replied blankly.

"Oh, right!" Aker said angrily. "You go cryin' to Rockwell, and he gets on our backs and—"

"And your pals get back in the starting lineup!" Jacobs finished. "What's the matter, big shot? Can't you stand on your own feet?"

CHAPTER 11

A Learning Experience

BEFORE CHIP HILTON could reply, Coach Ralston's "Let's go!" sent the starting team racing out on the field. Chip dug out for the referee who was waiting with the game ball on the thirty-five-yard line. Chip was shaking with anger. Now Jacobs and Aker were bringing Henry Rockwell into it! Well, he would show them whether or not he could stand on his own feet.

The official tossed the ball to him, and Chip placed it carefully on the tee. Then he turned quickly and headed straight for Speed. "Play the safety spot on this kickoff, Speed!" he said shortly. "I'm going to make the tackle." Before Speed had a chance to protest, Chip backpedaled to the thirty-yard line, signaled to the official that he was ready, and then concentrated on the ball.

The referee raised his arm, and a burst of cheers from the bleachers shot out toward him. Chip could scarcely wait for the whistle. Then the shrill blast cut through the crowd noise, and Chip started slowly toward the ball. He held back a little and got a little farther under the ball than usual, hoping that he would get a high kick that would carry the ball down to the vicinity of the five-yard line.

The drive of his leg carried him ahead of his teammates, and he sprinted at full speed. Skillfully evading one blocker after another, he drove straight for the visitors' receiver, who had caught the ball on his own five-yard line. Chip fended one more blocker away with his hands and then dove over the last one to drop the runner on the Mercer twelve-yard line.

Chip knew that the crowd's roar was a tribute to the tackle he had made, but that wasn't what was on his mind. He scurried back to the sidelines and up to Coach Ralston, his face grim and determined.

"Coach, I'd really like to play a few defensive series."

"The defense? You're the starting quarterback. What's this all about?"

"I think it would be a real learning experience, Coach."

Curly Ralston studied Chip's face for a brief moment and then looked down the sidelines at Aker and Jacobs. He nodded briefly and smiled. "One series."

Catching the nod and hearing the words "a few" from Coach Ralston, Chip raced back onto the field and joined the defensive unit.

Surprised, Mike Brennan remarked, "Nice tackle, Chip, but what are you doin' out here? What's Coach got on his mind?"

"He just wants me to have a learning experience, Mike," Chip said, putting his mouth guard in place.

Chip dropped into Ace Gibbons's outside linebacker position and waved the veteran back to the safety position. "Trade positions a couple of times, Ace. OK?"

"What's the idea? What's going on?" Ace asked curiously.

"I'll trade back on fourth down. All right?"

"Sure, it's all right," Gibbons said slowly, scanning Chip's face. He grasped Chip's arm. "Look, Chip! Don't let those two guys get to you. They're not worth it." He turned and trotted back to Chip's position as the Mercer offense broke their huddle and advanced to the line of scrimmage.

Chip was still seething as he moved almost automatically to the right and eyed the visitors' offensive set. The formation was unbalanced to the left, and Chip figured the play for an off-tackle smash or an end run. But something about the position of Mercer's left end caught his eye. Chip moved back a step.

When the center put the ball in play, the big end faked a shoulder block at Maxim and cut out for the sideline. Chip raced along, slightly behind the big player, anticipating the play. "Sideline pass to the outside," he breathed. "Tough."

The Mercer quarterback faked to his running back and then fired the ball to the tall end. The pass was angled for the sideline so that the receiver's body was between Chip and the ball. It was an ideal pass, tough to defend and almost impossible to intercept. Chip stretched his long legs and raced for the sideline. Timing his leap, he stretched his right hand as far as it would go.

The nose of the spinning ball bored into his eager fingers and slipped partly away. But he managed to pull it in and land in bounds, only inches away from the sideline. For a second he had to do a tightrope dance to get his balance, giving the Mercer quarterback a chance to follow his pass. He came racing headlong, but Chip caught him just right with a hard stiff-arm that knocked him to the ground. Two other tacklers spun off him as he drove along the sideline, past the fifteen, the ten, the five, and over the goal line.

Touchdown!

The cheers of the State fans were still ringing across the field when State broke from their huddle and got set for the point-after try. Then, with Speed holding the ball, Chip kicked the extra point, and State University led, 7-0.

The Mercer captain elected to receive, and again Chip drove the ball to the visitors' five-yard line. This time, Chip had company when he sprinted down the middle of the field.

Fireball Finley and Biggie Cohen were right behind him, and the three of them dove at the ball carrier at the same time, dropping him on the fifteen-yard line.

When his teammates broke out of the defensive huddle, Ace slapped Chip on the back and faded back to the safety position without a word. Chip waited impatiently for the visitors to come out of their huddle, moving restlessly along the line.

Mercer came out and formed their line over the ball, which was unbalanced to the left. Chip shifted to a position behind Joe Maxim. The play was a quick opener over left tackle with the left halfback carrying, and Chip met him head-on in the hole, stopping him cold on the line of scrimmage for no gain. Once more, he heard the crowd cheer from the bleachers as he hustled back into the defensive huddle.

"Second and ten, guys," Mike Brennan said tersely. "We've got 'em wired. Let's keep 'em that way. Heads up, here they come."

Ace shouldered Chip as they moved out of the huddle. "I like it back there; it's a great view," he said, grinning. "I hope they try to throw one in my direction. If they do and I intercept it, I'll show you some fancy open-field running."

"And I'll be blocking for you and won't be able to see," Chip said cheerfully.

He moved to the outside position in State's second line of defense and studied the formation. Noting that the formation was still unbalanced to the left, he divided his attention between the quarterback and the end. On the "three" count, the Mercer field general faked to the left halfback on a dive play and then to the fullback through the middle. He then dropped straight back. Chip wasn't sure who had the ball because the end passed Maxim up and drove straight for Mike Brennan.

Chip followed the end for two quick strides, but then he saw the left halfback fade out toward the sideline. "My zone!" Chip breathed. "And he's wide open!"

Groaning at his stupidity, he followed as fast as he could. The Mercer quarterback had outfoxed him; he'd used the big left end as a decoy, and Chip had fallen for the deception.

"Pass!" Brennan shouted.

It was too late for Chip to get behind the halfback, so he chased him at full speed, watching the speedy runner's eyes. But the halfback was clever; he never shifted his gaze. Chip was on the verge of turning his head to locate the ball when he heard Speed's frantic shout. "Chip! Now! Now!"

The warning came just in time. Seeing the halfback's eyes flash upward, Chip leaped and turned in the air. The ball was right over his head, and he made a desperate stab at the twirling pigskin. It was sheer luck, but his fingers managed to touch the ball just enough to change its trajectory and knock it out of bounds.

Angrily berating himself, Chip trotted back to the State huddle. "Tricked me," he said, glancing around the circle.

"No harm done," Ace said quickly. "You made a good play."

"Thanks to Speed," Chip said, glancing at his buddy.

"All right, all right!" Brennan said sharply. "Third and ten coming up! Let's try the double red dog blitz. For our new defensive teammate here, that's a 6-2-2-1 defense! Linebackers, let's get a good hard rush! Drop back, Chip."

Chip nodded his thanks to Ace and hurried back to the safety position on the thirty-five-yard line. But when Mercer came out of their huddle and lined up at the line of scrimmage, Chip, not wanting a receiver to get behind him for an easy catch, backpedaled a few more steps.

State's hard-charging linebackers rushed the passer, but before being dumped he managed to get the ball away, angling it toward his receiver, who was skirting down the left sideline. The defensive call worked! Chip saw the ball's flight and grabbed it in on the run before the Mercer receiver even realized there was nothing to catch.

Speed had dumped Mercer's right end, and Fireball had clobbered the center. Chip sprinted down the left sideline and reached the visitors' twenty-three-yard line before he was pulled down.

"Are we rolling!" Soapy exulted when they reached the huddle.

"Heads up, now!" Chip called. "First and ten! Formation right! Twenty-three draw play! Fireball on two! Break!"

After slipping the ball to Fireball, he cut back as if to pass. It was a good fake, but when he turned to look, there was a big pileup at the line of scrimmage. Fireball had run into a stone wall. He cast a quick look at the Mercer linemen as they unscrambled. They were big, rough, and tough!

Second and ten. The huddle formed, and Chip called for a pass. "The 90 R with a hook," he said calmly. "That's you, Monty. It'll be on your numbers on the ten-yard line. On one, guys!"

Chip faked to Fireball, who was diving into the line, and cut past Ace. Still concealing the ball, he faded back, but the fake didn't work.

The Mercer left tackle and left end barreled in at full speed, and Chip barely had time to get the ball away. Even at that, he hit Montague perfectly, drilling a hard, fast pass smack into the lanky end's stomach. But Montague dropped the ball. Third and ten.

The ball still rested on the twenty-three-yard stripe, ten yards in from the left sideline. Chip calculated the angle for a possible field-goal attempt. He decided to try one more running play. "Formation right! Reverse 59 to the right! Montague to Whittemore. Lots of good blocking now! On three! Break!"

Again Chip faked to Fireball and Gibbons. Then he slipped the ball to Montague and continued toward the visitors' left linebacker. It was the same play that had brought on the trouble with Jacobs, and Murph Kelly's advice about the use of a straight shoulder block burned vividly in Chip's mind. A fake cross-body block with his torso and shoulders drew the halfback's hands to Chip's left, and Chip drove through with a straight shoulder block that knocked his opponent cleanly to the ground.

The block carried Chip down on top of the halfback, and when he leaped to his feet and twisted around to look for Whitty, he saw that the big end was down on the twenty-five-yard line. Fourth down! And State had lost two yards in this series!

Chip was the farthest Statesman downfield, and his teammates stood waiting in the huddle. "Knock it down, Chip," Brennan urged.

"Right!" Chip said, nodding. "On two, guys! Break!"

Speed focused his thoughts and knelt in the holding position. On the "two" count Brennan's snap came back fast and true and straight into Speed's hands.

Chip took a short forward step with his right foot, then a long left. He met the ball with his kicking toe just as Speed plunked it on the ground. He could have made the kick blindfolded. Nobody, but nobody, could handle the ball for a placement better than Speed. The ball twirled end over end and straight through the middle of the uprights for three points. State 10, Mercer 0.

In an unusual twist even for a scrimmage, the Mercer captain elected to kick. Chip turned to lead the way to the receiving formation just as Gary Young, Aker, Jacobs, and Junior Roberts came trotting out on the field.

Without breaking his stride, Chip headed for the bench. Then he heard the applause and shouts and glanced up to see that the fans were standing and yelling and looking straight at him.

"Way to go, Hilton!"

"Nice going, kid!"

"That's the way, Hilton!"

Chip cast another quick look and located Skip. His new friend was standing in his usual place in the bleachers, yelling at him and shaking an exulting fist in the air. Chip sat down on the bench as Coach Ralston walked by.

With a Cheshire smile, Curly Ralston remarked, "Hope *your* learning experience got through to *them.*"

Skip was one of the last of the fans to sit down, but that didn't diminish his enthusiasm. He turned gloatingly to Mr. Aker and Mr. Jacobs.

"What did you think of *that* performance?" he demanded.

"What performance?" Mr. Aker repeated. "What did he do?"

"Do? Oh, Chip just kicked off and made the tackle, intercepted a pass and ran for a touchdown, kicked the extra point, kicked off again and helped make the tackle, played in a defensive position and made the first tackle from scrimmage, knocked down an almost sure pass, ran back an interception for twenty-seven yards, and kicked a field goal. That's all he did!"

"Showoff!" Mr. Aker said sourly.

Coach Bill Carpenter and Mr. Blaine had scarcely spoken to the two men until then. But Carpenter couldn't resist the temptation to join the conversation. "That's right," he agreed blandly. "He sure did show off his football talents. He showed what an all-American quarterback—no, what an all-American player—can do! Now we'll see what *your* kids can do."

CHAPTER 12

The Value and Values of Sports

"OUR KIDS will do all right," Mr. Jacobs said hotly. "Trouble is, they don't call the plays like Hilton does."

"No one does that," Skip agreed, grinning.

"Hilton never gives our kids a chance!" Ed Aker growled. "He *never* calls their signals."

"Hilton isn't calling the signals *now,*" Mr. Blaine said calmly.

"Right!" Jacobs agreed. "Now you'll see some team play. Young called the plays for the freshman team last year, and I guess *they* did all right."

"Sure did!" Aker added. "Won every game!"

"Hilton tries to do everything," Jacobs complained. "He's always putting on a show, trying to do everything himself."

"Mark my words," Aker said. "Young will make everyone forget Hilton if Ralston gives him a chance. We've seen him work."

Carpenter burst into a gale of laughter. "You must be crazy," he said. "Young's a nice kid, but he can't carry Hilton's shoes. He can't run or pass or kick half as well as Hilton.

Besides, he's not as big or fast or half as smart! And another thing, Aker, Hilton doesn't *try* to do everything. He *does* everything!"

"But good!" Skip added.

"No, my friend," Carpenter continued, "no one will forget Hilton for a long, long time. Skip here is tops in our league and plays a lot of football, but he's far from being another Hilton."

"Give him time," Blaine said shortly, glancing at his nephew. "Wait until Skip gets two years of Brand football under his belt and two years under Stew Peterson."

"Chip is more than a football player," Skip said quickly. "He's a top student. He leads his class."

"Our kids aren't dummies by a long shot," Jacobs growled. "Hilton hasn't got a monopoly on brains."

"What about your idea of the triple-threat triplets?" Mr. Blaine asked pointedly. "The first time we met you two men, that was all you talked about—Hilton and your kids being the triple-threat triplets."

"Humph!" Aker snorted. "You think Hilton's gonna let anyone touch the ball? Not a chance! We didn't know Hilton then, but we know him now. Our kids tell us what goes on."

The conversation ended as Mercer kicked the ball. It hurtled high into the air and down to State's receiver, Junior Roberts, on the ten-yard line. There he was tackled so hard that the official called a time-out. Murph Kelly worked on the big fullback for a few moments before play resumed.

Back-up quarterback Gary Young tried an off-tackle slant to the right, with Aker carrying, for no gain. Then the little quarterback called on Jacobs for a wide-end run around the other side of the line. But the sharp blocking of the starting backs was noticeable by its absence, and Jacobs was thrown for a five-yard loss back on the five-yard line.

Young was desperate and tried a short pass over the middle which the Mercer linebacker nearly intercepted. It was fourth and fifteen now, and State had to kick.

The visitors' ends broke through Aker's and Jacobs's weak blocks, but Roberts got a good kick away, booting the ball to the Mercer forty-five-yard line. Biggie Cohen dropped the receiver in his tracks.

On the sidelines, the State coaching staff held true to their game plan of giving some players work on both the offense and the defense. This was the final scrimmage before returning to workouts at University Stadium, and the coaches wanted to evaluate each player's skills. From this scrimmage, players would be ranked position by position in the depth chart.

The visitors had learned all they needed to know about State's veteran line by this time, so they took to the air. The first pass was in Aker's territory, and the visitors' right end went high in the air over Aker's head and came down with the ball on the State thirty-five-yard line. Aker's tackle was late, and the end bulled his way for five more yards before he went down.

A short buttonhook in front of Jacobs was good for ten yards, and the visitors had the ball on the State twenty. Brennan waited until the huddle formed to call time out. Then, Ralston sent Finley, Gibbons, and Morris racing in for Roberts, Aker, and Jacobs. Chip quickly got to his feet, but the coach looked right past him. Chip sank back down onto the bench. He remained there for the rest of the game.

The State veterans' strong defense stalled Mercer's running and passing attack, but without Chip to spark their own offense, the Statesmen could do no more than play the visitors on even terms. There was no more scoring, and when the game ended, Chip joined his friends and walked along with them toward the cabins.

"One of those Mercer guys asked if I was related to some guy named Red Grange," Soapy said smugly.

"Soapy, have you ever even heard the name 'Red Grange' before?" Speed needled.

Soapy reddened. "No, but it sounded like a compliment."

"Well, not to Red Grange," Speed laughed. "Red Grange was a famous NFL Hall of Fame back."

"And," Biggie added, "an all-American selection in the 1920s."

"I'd be all-American, too," Soapy growled, "if Ralston used *me* where I belong."

"Where's that?"

"In the backfield!"

"You can't run fast enough to catch a cold," Schwartz joked.

"Well, anyway," Soapy said loftily, "I bet I look like that Red Grange guy."

"Give it up, Soapy," Speed said. "Grange was six-two and could run like a deer. Besides, he was as lean as a greyhound."

"Well," Soapy conceded, "maybe I can't run like Grange could and maybe I'm not a greyhound—"

Speed couldn't let that pass. "You hear that, Biggie?" he cried. "Soapy says he's not a greyhound."

"Of course he isn't," Biggie drawled. "He's a chowhound."

That set Speed off on another gale of laughter that made him double over and hold his stomach. Soapy waited grimly until Speed straightened up and quieted down and then continued slowly, choosing his words carefully. "I meant to say that I'm not as lean as a greyhound, but I'm like him—"

"Like a greyhound! Oh, no!"

"No!" Soapy shouted in exasperation. "Like Red Grange! I wear number 77 and I've got red hair."

Roaring with laughter, Speed and Biggie jumped on the redhead and roughed him up all the way to the cabin. Chip had enjoyed the kidding, but he wanted to be ready in plenty of time for the trip to University. He hustled off to take his shower. The rest of his friends followed suit and then carried their gear outside.

A few minutes later the bus appeared, and Soapy grabbed his duffel bags. "C'mon, you guys!" he yelled. "Let's go! University, here we come!"

It was a hilarious ride. The end of training camp had released the players from most of their tension, and since Mr. Aker and Mr. Jacobs had driven their sons home, there was nothing to dampen the enthusiasm of the squad. Soapy took charge, suggesting and leading cheers for everyone in the bus, including the driver.

Then he suggested a round of good-natured boos for the coaches, and the response was so enthusiastic that several of the sophomores riding in the back seat cast apprehensive glances back at the coaches' car, which was right behind the bus.

There wasn't much levity in the coaches' car. Curly Ralston was in a glum mood, his attitude clearly expressing his disappointment in the showing of the Statesmen against Mercer.

"They were pretty big," Nelson said tentatively.

"And tough!" Sullivan added. "I hope we don't run into another line like that. Not this season anyway."

"It wasn't their *line,*" Ralston said gloomily. "It was *our* depth, or rather our lack of it. If Aker and Jacobs would only team up with Hilton, we might be able to get by. If they don't—"

"It *could* be a dream backfield," Nelson said.

"You mean nightmare backfield," Sullivan growled. "For Hilton and us too. I haven't had a good night's sleep since those two reported to camp."

"I guess we'll all be glad to get back to University," Rockwell said softly.

Since Coach Ralston had not scheduled a practice for the first day of the semester, Chip hurried down to his job at Grayson's to try to catch up on a whole summer's accumulation of stockroom problems. His task was doubly challenging because his assistant, Isaiah Redding, had been given other duties.

Chip glanced at the stockroom clock. Eight o'clock and two more hours to go. It had been a long, long day. His first class had met at eight o'clock that Monday morning, and he had waded through all the hustle and bustle of starting new classes, meeting old friends, and getting back into the swing of college life.

The highlight of his day, however, had been an invitation to attend a civic luncheon from a friend at the *Herald*. Chip smiled as he recalled Bill Bell's pleased expression when the sportswriter had tried to introduce Chip to the guest speaker, Mr. H. L. Armstrong.

The big speaker had laughed and extended his hand. "No need for introductions here, Bill. I know Chip Hilton! He's an old summer employee of the Mansfield Steel Company and a star pitcher on our summer-league baseball team. And from what my daughter Peggy tells me, which isn't much, she and Chip E-mail each other on a regular basis."

Chip enjoyed seeing Mr. Armstrong again, but what really impressed him was his luncheon address to University's civic leaders on "The Value and Values of Sports at the Community Level."

Chip spent most of the afternoon and evening reflecting on Mr. Armstrong's message. It seemed to Chip that parents and coaches in a community could accomplish an awful lot in helping kids to learn skills and develop positive character traits and habits through their youth sports programs. Then it struck him. This idea was just like what his dad had created in their backyard in Valley Falls so many years ago. The Hilton Athletic Club (Hilton A. C.) had given Chip those values! And his friends had joined the fun too. All of the Valley Falls crowd were longtime members of the Hilton A. C. This *was* an organization he hoped he could somehow be part of.

His thoughts were stopped short by a loud thump as Soapy lumbered through the stockroom door and dropped wearily into a chair.

"What a crowd!" the redhead said. "Everybody in town must have been waiting for us to get back. Chip, we weren't as busy as this last year after the A & M game! Oh, my aching back and feet!"

"How about Fireball and Whitty?"

"We're taking turns for a breather. They'll be in as soon as I finish my break. Oh, I almost forgot! Skip Miller is out there. Want to see him?"

"Sure!" Chip said. "Sit still. I'll get him."

Skip was perched on a stool at the end of the crowded fountain, sipping a cherry Coke. But he finished his drink with a quick gulp as soon as he saw Chip.

He hopped off the stool and extended his hand. "I hope I'm not taking you away from anything," Skip said nervously.

"You're not," Chip said quickly, shaking the high school athlete's hand. "Come on back."

When they reached the stockroom, Skip placed a piece of paper in Chip's hand. "Trouble," he said, shaking his head worriedly. "It's a letter of intent for Brand University. Uncle Merton wants me to sign it."

"An intent letter?"

"That's right. He says they're offering me a football scholarship."

"Why sign it now?"

Skip shook his head. "I don't know. Uncle Merton said it should be in early to show my commitment. What am I going to do?"

"Let's think about it," Chip said, studying the form.

"That isn't the only one," Skip said, pulling a sheaf of papers out of his pocket. "I've received about thirty letters from schools all over the country. You must have gotten a thousand!"

"Not quite," Chip said, smiling. "By the way, did all the letters generally contain information about the school's academic and football programs?"

Skip shook his head. "No. In fact, Chip, a few of the people who talked to me made all kinds of promises. They weren't

BRAND UNIVERSITY
Letter of Intent

Dear Sir,

I wish to indicate my intent to attend Brand University and accept a football scholarship at Brand University. If this award is approved, I agree to report for football on the date stipulated by the Conference and Brand University.

It is my understanding from the representative of Brand University who interviewed me that:

1. The scholarship awarded by the University will cover (a) tuition (b) fees (c) meals (d) dormitory housing (e) books.

2. I understand that any other aid afforded me by school officials, alumni, or friends to attend college or to influence my preference of college is prohibited and will render me ineligible.

3. If injured while participating in athletics supervised by a member of the coaching staff, the medical expenses will be paid by the athletic department.

4. This grant-in-aid is awarded for four years at Brand University as long as I conduct myself under the rules of the University, make normal progress toward graduation, and maintain a satisfactory grade point average.

Signature of Parent____________________________

Signature of Applicant____________________________

coaches. Alumni or fans, I guess you would call them, like Uncle Merton. Some of them promised me stuff like a car or money or better jobs for my parents. One man even said he would see that my family got a house, all paid for. I'm all mixed up."

Soapy had listened without saying a word. Now he couldn't stand it any longer. "*You're* all mixed up," he said unhappily. "Man, you ought to be in our shoes! State's touchdown twins have all of us in an uproar!"

The stockroom phone rang then. Chip answered and listened briefly. "Sure," he said. "Right away."

He turned to Skip. "I've got some work to do now, Skip. Why don't you hold off your uncle for a week or so? Maybe we can think of something. All right?"

"He's pretty hard to say no to, Chip, but I'll try." Skip started to move toward the door but then stopped. He licked his lips apprehensively and asked shyly, "You didn't have a chance to ask Mr. Grayson about a job, did you?"

"Not yet, Skip, but don't worry. I won't forget, I promise."

After Skip left, Soapy went back to the fountain counter in the food court area, and Chip began to input the latest inventory into the store's computer system.

Soapy, Fireball, and Whitty quit at ten o'clock sharp and left for Pete's Place around the corner to get a sandwich as the busy day wound down. Chip remained on the job, trying to get a head start for the next evening. He was so absorbed in his work that he didn't notice his employer standing in the open doorway to the stockroom.

George Grayson was in his fifties, tall and slender. His face was kind, and his hair was graying at the temples. He watched Chip quietly for a moment, a slight smile on his lips. "You can't do it all at once. You do need to sleep."

Chip was startled. He glanced up quickly and nodded. "I guess you're right, Mr. Grayson, but I'm pretty far behind."

"I guess you heard about Isaiah's promotion."

"Yes, sir. Mitzi told me about it. That's really great!"

Chip was truly happy for Isaiah and remembered when he had first come to work at Grayson's. Isaiah Redding lived in a tough neighborhood and had overcome some pretty tall challenges to work at the store. Chip was proud of him. Grayson smiled. "Yes, thanks to your training, Isaiah is now Mitzi's assistant. He helps her at the cash register. This is his day off. And don't worry, I'll find a replacement for him in a day or two."

"I know one, Mr. Grayson," Chip said eagerly. "A good one! That is, I think he will be a good one. He's a nice kid."

"What's his name?"

Chip hesitated. "Well, his last name is Miller. I forget his first name, but everyone calls him Skip, Skip Miller. He's quite a high school football player and he needs a job, badly."

Grayson nodded. "Skip Miller. Oh, yes. I've read about him in the *Herald*. Where did you meet him?"

It was a golden opportunity, and Chip seized it quickly. George Grayson was a sports fan. He liked collegiate athletics and having dedicated athletes working for him, but he never exploited their popularity. Nor did he pamper them. Chip held nothing back. He told his employer everything he knew about Skip and the young man's predicament.

When Chip finished, Grayson nodded and stated quietly, "Seems like he's in rather a tough spot, isn't he?"

"He sure is, Mr. Grayson," Chip breathed.

Grayson studied Chip's anxious face for a brief moment.

"Well," he said, "it looks as if Skip Miller has found a true friend." He paused briefly. "And," he added gently, "a job! Tell him to report to work as soon as he completes the paperwork."

CHAPTER 13

The White Helmet

SKIP MILLER caught the box of paper cups in his long, deft fingers and placed it on the stockroom shelf. "Keep 'em coming, Chip," he called, grinning.

"Don't worry," Chip replied, glancing at the big packing box. "There's plenty more."

When the box was emptied of its contents and the shelves neatly filled with supplies for the food court and pharmacy, the two new friends took a breather. Chip sat down at his desk, and Skip stretched out in a chair in the corner, sighing with contentment. "This has been a big week in my life, Chip," he said happily. "I've never had a real regular job before. If I could keep this job, I could go to State University and help out at home too. If only Uncle Merton would leave me alone."

"There's lots of time," Chip assured him.

Skip shook his head. "Uh-uh, that's where you're wrong. He keeps after me to sign that letter every time he sees me."

"Well, anyway," Chip replied, "the job gives you a measure of independence."

"You can say that again," Skip agreed, grinning. "My dad and mom are really happy too."

"How will it feel tomorrow when you get your first check?"

Skip grinned. "Like a million! How will you feel when you line up in the stadium tomorrow afternoon against Templeton?"

"The same way you'll feel next Friday night. Better than a million!"

"Bill Bell wrote in his column in the *Herald* this afternoon that Ralston plans to start the touchdown twins. Is that right?"

"I don't know, Skip. Coach has been working with them a lot this week."

"Bell said something else," Skip said, eyeing Chip carefully.

"What?"

"He said the fans would be watching for the first State player or players to run out on the field with a ball. Bell said he or they would be the new State captain or captains. He said that one of the players would be wearing number 44, your number."

"Don't believe everything you read in the papers."

"You'll see," Skip said confidently. "What are you writing?"

"Coach Ralston's new formation," Chip said.

"Mind if I look?"

"Of course not."

Chip had drawn the right and left shifts of the formation and written in the names of the best players. The only exceptions had been the right end and the two halfback positions.

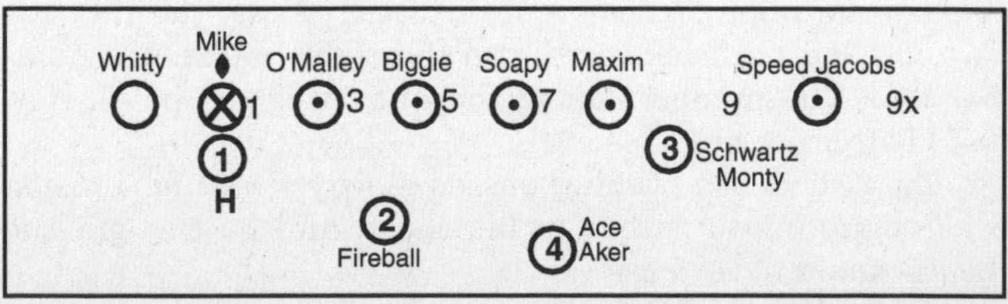

"We're using almost the same formation," Skip said thoughtfully. "I thought Speed and Jacobs alternated in the left-halfback positions—"

"They do," Chip explained. "But that's where Coach Ralston uses his halfbacks. He shifts the left halfback to the right-end position on formation right and his right halfback to the left-end position when the shift is to the left."

"Where does the right end play?"

Chip pointed to Red Schwartz's name. "Right here. A yard behind the line and just off Maxim's right shoulder."

"How about the left formation?"

Chip quickly sketched the formation and wrote in the names. "Do you get it?" he asked.

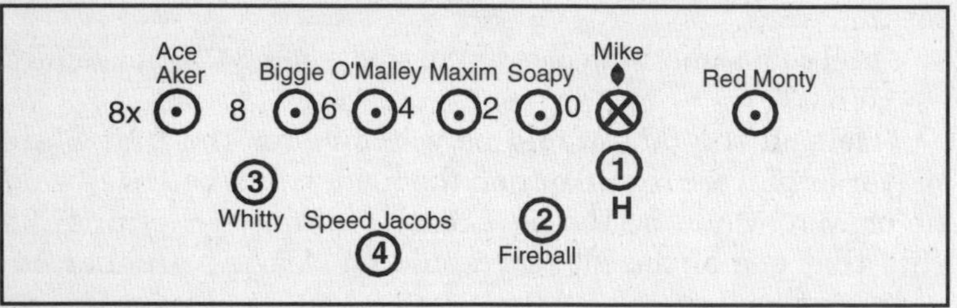

"I still don't understand why he uses the halfbacks in the end positions," Skip said, shaking his head.

"He sometimes spreads the ends," Chip explained, "and that puts our backs out wide where their speed is important. Besides, the ends are used for the heavy blocking on the running plays, and being positioned a yard back gives them a little more authority when they hit."

"How do you call the plays?"

"By the numbers. The quarterback is one, the fullback two, the left halfback three, and the right halfback is number four. The numbers along the line show the holes. Hey, we'd better get busy."

The rest of the evening passed slowly for Chip. Tension was beginning to gather in his chest, and he thought the hours would never pass.

The sun was shining brightly the next morning. There was a bit of a breeze, but it was a perfectly glorious football day. Chip worked nonstop on the computer in the stockroom until noon, and when he left for the stadium, he was as nervous as when he had played his very first collegiate game.

Murph Kelly and his assistant trainers taped each player quickly and efficiently and then hustled them into the locker room where their uniforms were laid out. Chip dressed slowly and carefully, checking each part of his uniform over and over. Just as he finished, Coach Ralston and his assistants appeared in the doorway. Murph Kelly hastily cleared his throat and called the players to order.

"This isn't going to be a pep talk," Ralston said, scanning the eager faces of his players. "However, there *is* one important task to be performed before we go out on the field: the selection of a captain or captains. All right, Murph, hand out the pencils and paper ballots."

Chip quickly wrote "Ace Gibbons" at the top and "Mike Brennan" at the bottom and folded it neatly. After a minute or so Murph Kelly collected the papers in a helmet and placed it on the table in front of Ralston. Then, with Rockwell, Nelson, and Sullivan helping him, Coach Ralston sorted the papers.

At the end, there were only four stacks. One lone piece of paper lay in three of them and all the others stood in one big pile. A little smile hovered on the lips of the coach as he faced the squad. "You have chosen only one player as your overall team captain," he said. "He won both offensive and defensive leaderships, hands down."

Ralston turned to pick up the traditional white helmet with the blue stripe and red letters. He held it briefly in his hands, commenting on the many young men who had held this leadership honor.

Then he tossed it quickly and surely into Chip's hands. His "Good luck, Hilton" was lost in a cheer that shook the room. Chip placed the symbolic helmet on top of his locker and turned to thank his teammates.

Minutes later, carrying the ball under his arm, Chip led the starting team onto the field and was met with a deafening roar from the State University fans. Chip's heart was thumping so hard he felt as though he would never get his breath. But the feeling disappeared when he trotted out to the center of the field with Ace Gibbons, Mike Brennan, and Biggie Cohen. The four officials waited there.

Four Templeton players ran out from the visitors' bench at the same time. The referee took care of the introductions and then turned to the Templeton players. "Visitors' choice, men. Heads or tails?"

The tallest of the four players said, "Heads." Heads it was, and the same player chose to defend the north goal.

"We'll receive," Chip stated decisively.

While the referee was signaling the choices to the stands, Chip shook hands with the visiting field captains and wished them luck. Pivoting, he ran back to the circle of players surrounding Ralston.

"All right," the coach said, extending his hand. "We're receiving. Remember, they've got the wind behind them. Good luck!"

Chip and his teammates trotted out to their positions, and the roar of the crowd and the chords of the State University fight song came beating down around them until Chip couldn't distinguish the State cheers from those of the Templeton fans.

The captain was pleased—but also surprised—that Coach Ralston had called his number for the kickoff unit. He glanced quickly toward Jacobs on his left and Aker on his right as the Templeton kicker placed the ball on the tee at the other end of the field. Now that Coach Ralston had started them in the first game of the season, he wondered if they would forget their animosity toward him and play team football. He knew it wouldn't take him long to find out.

The referee raised his hand, and Chip acknowledged the signal. On the blast of the whistle, the Templeton kicker started forward, picked up his line of teammates, and booted the ball high into the air. But he tried to get the ball too far up in the air, and it carried only as far as Finley, who was standing on his own twenty-yard line. Fireball took the ball and headed bull-like straight up the middle. And he didn't vary his path an inch, plowing straight away until he went down under a swarm of tacklers on the State thirty-two-yard line. It had been a quick twelve-yard return.

Chip followed swiftly and was already in the huddle position when Fireball was uncovered by the referee. He wanted to be sure that Aker and Jacobs got the feel of a real game before entrusting them with the ball and called on Fireball for a draw play over right guard. "Formation right! Twenty-three on three!" he said. "That's you, Fireball. Let's go!"

Fireball bulled his way to the thirty-seven-yard line, and it was second down, with five yards to go. Chip glanced at Aker and met the steady gaze of the right halfback. "Forty-four on two! That's you, Aker! Cross buck! Fake to Fireball as you cross. Let's go!"

Chip faked to Fireball with his left hand and held the ball on his thigh with his right hand. As he passed Aker, he gave him the ball and continued on back to his passing position. Aker took the ball at full speed and carried to the forty-three-yard line for the first down. Back in the huddle, Chip smiled at him and nodded his head. "Nice going, Aker."

"Thanks, captain, *sir!*" Aker said, a mocking smile on his lips.

It was all Chip could do to take the thinly veiled insult, but he did it, filing the little incident away for future reference. But, even as he called the play, he was thinking that the feud was still uppermost in Aker's mind.

"Heads up!" he said quickly. "Formation right! Thirty-eight on one! That's you, Jacobs, on the reverse. Break!"

Chip took the ball from Brennan on the one count, faked to Finley and then Aker, and slipped the ball to Jacobs as the left halfback raced back out of the right-end position. Jacobs picked up good interference from Soapy and O'Malley and carried the ball to the Templeton forty-five-yard line before he was downed. It was a twelve-yard gain and another first down.

The State fans were rooting the Statesmen on with their "Go! Go! Go!" cheer, and Chip could hardly make himself heard in the huddle. He called the play and looked around the circle of faces. From their huddle positions directly in front of him, Aker and Jacobs were openly sneering, secure in the fact that no one but Chip could see their faces.

The "I told you so" expressions on the faces of the touchdown twins were hard to take. For a split second, Chip was on the verge of telling them off. But, once again, he passed over their animosity and called the play. "Formation left!" he said, covering up the short interlude in his thinking. "Thirty-two on three! That's you again, Jacobs. Cross buck. Break!"

"Thank you, captain, *sir,*" Jacobs said, smirking and glancing slyly at Aker.

"Check!" Chip cried. "Signals off!" He turned quickly to the referee. "Time!"

CHAPTER 14

A Hand in the Victory

MOST OF THE STATESMEN had started for the line. They walked back now, some of them with curiosity written on their faces, others with grim understanding and hope. Soapy, Biggie, Fireball, Whitty, and Brennan were in the latter group. Chip had taken all he could stomach from Aker and Jacobs. This thing was going to be settled right there and then.

He strode into the middle of the circle of players and held up his hand for silence. "Let's get this squared away once and for all," he said grimly. "I didn't ask for it, but you guys elected me your captain. Also, Coach told you why the quarterback runs the team. From now on, there will be no more wisecracks or talking in the huddle by anyone unless it concerns a play."

Chip paused and moved directly in front of Aker and Jacobs. He looked from one to the other as he continued. "As for you two, the next time you give me that 'mister' or 'sir' or any other funny stuff—on the middle of the field or in the huddle—you're leaving the game or *I* am. Understand?"

The touchdown twins faced up to him for a long second. Then their bravado broke and they nodded sullenly. They shifted their eyes and glanced briefly at each other before stepping back.

Chip took his place in the huddle, angrily aware of the cold hate showing in the eyes of Aker and Jacobs as they glared at him. “All right,” he said, forcing himself to ignore the bitter duo, “same play. Thirty-two on three! Let’s go!”

There wasn’t a sound from the players as they whirled out of the huddle and hustled up to the line. As the quarterback and captain, Chip considered going to the sidelines for two subs to replace Aker and Jacobs. But he decided against the idea, hoping his talk in the huddle was sufficient. He faked to Fireball, slipped the ball to Jacobs, and dropped back, again faking a pass.

Jacobs cut between Brennan and Montague and carried three yards to the Templeton forty-two-yard line.

At second and seven, Chip called for the right formation and pass takeoff from the fake crossing of the backs. It worked perfectly. Fireball drove through the line as if he were carrying for a touchdown, and Aker did the same. When Chip faded back this time, he had the ball.

Montague had sprinted out into the right flat, and Chip could have hit him. But Jacobs had cut through the line, broken toward the middle of the field, and then headed for the sideline. He was in the clear, speeding past the Templeton twenty-yard line. Chip gave him a good lead, aiming the ball for the ten-yard line.

It was a beautiful pass: timed just right, light as a fleecy cloud, and perfectly placed. It was hard to miss, a perfect touchdown pass. Perhaps Jacobs was too anxious; maybe he was surprised Chip would throw to him after the huddle episode.

Whatever the reason, Jacobs leaped too soon, got only a piece of the ball, and couldn’t hold on to it. The once sure catch bounced off his fingertips and right into the hands of the visitors' defender! The speedy runner was surprised, but he recovered instantly and took off straight up the sideline.

Never dreaming Jacobs would miss the pass, Chip had drifted over to the right sideline to cover. He groaned and dashed up behind Montague, trying desperately to get into position for a good tackle. But three of the Templeton secondary players had immediately formed ahead of the ball carrier and were leading him up the sideline. One of them bowled Montague over, and the other two concentrated on Chip.

He tried to bluff a block so they would show first, but neither left his feet. The ball carrier reached him then, and it was now or never.

Chip dove over the first blocker and managed to grasp the runner's jersey. But the second blocker had delayed just long enough and had a clear shot at Chip. He cut Hilton down from the side with a vicious cross-body block just as the runner sped past and headed for the goal line.

Chip was up almost as soon as he was down and gave chase. But the runner was tearing across the fifty-yard line, twenty yards ahead, and it was an impossible handicap. Chip managed to pick up ten of the twenty yards, but that was as close as he could get. The ball carrier crossed the goal line to score the first touchdown of the game. Just a few seconds later, the visitors' placekicker booted a perfect placement.

The score: Templeton 7, State 0.

State University elected to receive again, disappointed and hurt by the sudden twist of fate that had changed a sure State touchdown into a score for Templeton. But it was past and Chip waited eagerly for the Templeton kick. The visitors still had the wind behind them, and he figured the kick this time would carry all the way to the goal line. He was right. The whistle bit through the crowd roar, and the ball was in the air, heading straight toward him.

He shot a quick glance toward the wave of tacklers. Aker and Jacobs made weak attempts to block the rangy ends who converged on him, but the eager Templeton wing men of the kickoff squad ran over them as if they weren't there. Chip didn't have a chance and barely made it to the twelve-yard line before he was smashed to the ground.

He was furious when he scrambled to his feet. It was the same old story! Aker and Jacobs would put out when they carried the ball or went out for a pass, but they weren't going to block or tackle—for the team or State or Ralston or anyone else.

After three unproductive downs, Chip punted on the fourth to the visitors' forty-yard line. The State defense held Templeton there for no gain. The game developed into a kicking contest until there were only four minutes left to play in the second quarter. State now had the ball on their own forty-yard line.

Chip threw five consecutive passes. The Statesmen had moved to the Templeton eighteen-yard line through the air. On second down, with four to go, Chip passed to Montague. The slender end pulled in the ball, but two of the Templeton players hit him so hard that he fumbled, and the visitors recovered it. Again, errors had stalled State's momentum. With less than a minute to play, Templeton held onto the ball, and two plays later the period ended. The score at the half: Templeton 7, State 0.

State controlled the ball through the third quarter, but they couldn't score. In the last quarter, with State in possession on their own forty-five-yard line, Ralston sent in all his offensive unit veterans and Chip opened up.

Using his best sequence series, Chip sent Fireball through the middle for six yards. Ace picked up three yards, but he hurt his knee on the play and had to be carried from the field. When time was in, Speed, replacing the injured Ace, cut through right tackle for five.

It was first and ten on the Templeton forty-one-yard line, and on the way back to the huddle, Chip figured the visitors were ripe for a pass. "Formation right! Double reverse pass!

To Monty, to Whitty, and back to me! Keep going, Monty! On two! Break!"

It was a difficult play, but everything clicked. Chip faked to Fireball and then to Aker, slipped the ball to Montague, and faded back. Montague drove to the left and handed the ball to Whittemore. Whitty raced toward the right and then lateraled to Chip, who faked a pass to Speed and then saw Fireball swerve to the left in front of the goal. He aimed the ball for the corner of the end zone, and Fireball pulled it in with a tremendous leap. State was back in the ball game!

A few seconds later Chip hit Whittemore with a basketball toss over the line for the two-point play, and the Statesmen took the lead, 8-7.

The State fans were deliriously happy. The Statesmen's lead had been a long time in coming. Templeton chose to receive and sent in fresh players for their receiving team. The visitors' coach had substituted freely all through the game, whereas Ralston had made only a few replacements on offense and defense. Now he decided to give Morris and Montague a rest and replaced them with Jacobs and Schwartz. The Statesmen got a standing ovation as they trotted back to line up for the kick.

Chip groaned to himself when Travis Aker came in to replace Speed. The touchdown twins were both in again! One was bad enough! He glanced at the clock. Five minutes . . .

The visitors went to their air attack and moved the ball to the fifty-yard line. State held them, and Templeton was forced to kick. Chip caught the ball on the State goal line and was downed on his own five. There were only three minutes to play!

Chip wanted to use up the clock. Calling on the same group of plays he had used at the start of the game, Chip sent Fireball barreling through the middle for five yards and then shifted right and used Aker for the well-established diagonal crossing with Finley for three. If his strategy was right, Templeton would be expecting Jacobs on the wide reverse. He glanced at the clock. Forty seconds remained, and Templeton had used all of their time-outs!

Back in the huddle Chip concentrated on Aker as he called the play. "Formation right! Nineteen keeper on two! I need a good fake, Aker! Let's go!"

On the "two" count Chip took Brennan's snap, pivoted to the right, and faked to Fireball. Then he clamped the ball on his thigh with his right hand and faked to Aker with his left. Fireball and Aker covered up beautifully. Still clutching the ball tightly against his thigh with his right hand, Chip slowed and started his fake to Jacobs.

The Templeton linebackers shifted toward the other side, and the visitors' defensive captain shouted, "Reverse! Watch the reverse!"

Chip's heart leaped. It had worked! He was away, free and clear! He shot a quick glance ahead. The visitors' end had dropped back a step, and Soapy was just pulling out of the line and heading toward him.

Just as he finished the last fake, Chip started his sprint. Then it happened! For no apparent reason, Jacobs made a grab for the hidden ball. It went spinning out of Chip's hands, bobbing and bouncing back toward the State goal line. Why Jacobs would make such a move was too much for Chip to take in. All he knew was that the ball was gone and he was chasing it.

"Ball!" he cried.

The Templeton left end hit Chip from behind and knocked him to the ground. The big player dove for the ball; but he was too eager, and his clutching fingers sent it spiraling farther in the direction of the goal line. The ball was loose and wobbled across the goal line and into the end zone.

Chip groaned in dismay as a Templeton player fell on the elusive pigskin just as the clock hit 00:00, ending the game.

The referee's arms shot over his head. Touchdown!

The fans on the visitors' side of the stadium were going wild as Chip got slowly to his feet, still trying to figure out why Jacobs had tried to grab the ball. It was fantastically unbelievable that a starting varsity player had misunderstood the play. Then he heard Whitty's shout.

"I saw you!" Whittemore shouted angrily, charging toward Jacobs. "You grabbed that ball on purpose! What's wrong with you?"

The referee stepped between the two State players, but that didn't stop Whittemore. The big end was beyond reasoning. His face was livid with rage, and he brushed the official aside as if he were made of air. Before anyone could stop him, Whittemore was on Jacobs, swinging with all his might.

Chip ran toward Whitty and locked his arms. Biggie joined him a second later. It was all they could do to pull the infuriated giant away.

Then, just when Whittemore had calmed down somewhat, and while Chip and Biggie were still holding his arms, Travis Aker smashed his right fist into Whittemore's mouth, cutting Whitty's lip and sending the blood flying.

Soapy went into action then. He grabbed Aker from behind, wrestled him roughly to the ground, and sat on him. It was a mad, whirling, mixed-up skirmish, and the Templeton players watched the unfolding scene in amazement.

Coaches Ralston, Rockwell, Sullivan and half of the State players were out on the field, trying to help the angry officials.

"Get those players off the field," the referee demanded as he tossed his flag into the air for unsportsmanlike conduct. He pointed toward Whittemore, Aker, and Jacobs. "All of them! Out!"

Whittemore was raving again, trying to escape from Chip's and Biggie's restraining arms. The angry end was intent on reaching Aker, but Sullivan and Rockwell grasped his arms and led him off the field. Ralston followed with Aker and Jacobs.

A second later, March, Young, and Montague raced out and reported for the three banished players. Chip glanced at the bench and saw that Rockwell, Sullivan, and Murph Kelly were escorting Whitty, Aker, and Jacobs along the sideline toward the players' exit.

The angry referee plunked the ball down on the grass in front of the State goal. "Play ball!" he growled. "Line up to try for the extra point."

Fighting mad, baffled, and frustrated, the demoralized Statesmen manned the scrimmage line. They rose up to stop an off-tackle smash, but it didn't change anything. The game was over, and Jacobs had handed Templeton a victory and the first big upset of the season. The final score: Templeton 13, State 8.

CHAPTER 15

Flying and Football

"WHAT HAPPENED?" Biggie asked as the defeated Statesmen walked slowly from the field.

"I don't know," Chip said dully. "Jacobs must have gotten mixed up."

"Oh, sure!" Soapy said bitterly. "He was mixed up, all right! Thought he was playing for Templeton! Mixed up enough to spoil the play. He did it on *purpose.* Just like Whitty said. I saw him grab the ball. He wasn't mixed up."

"Soapy's right," Ace Gibbons added emphatically. "We even saw it from the bench."

"Chip was specific enough about the play in the huddle," Brennan said. "He called the nineteen keeper play. Jacobs knew—"

"It was a gift!" Gibbons raged.

"On a platter!" Fireball growled.

"Yeah," Brennan added. "Served up by State's famous touchdown twins."

"Coach shoulda known better," O'Malley growled.

When he reached the locker room, Chip dropped down on a bench between Soapy and Fireball and slowly began to take off his uniform. Across the way he could hear shouts and cheers and the joyful celebration in the Templeton locker room, but there were no cheers or yells or good-natured gibes here. He was pulling the tape from his ankles when Murph Kelly bellowed for silence. "Coach wants to say something."

Coaches Ralston and Rockwell were waiting quietly in the center of the big room. "All right, men," Ralston said in an even tone as he glanced from player to player. "It was a tough one to lose. We had some bad breaks today, but we were beaten by a better team. The only satisfaction I have from this game is that you gave all you had, and that's all anyone can ask.

"Fortunately, it was a nonconference game, but it's hard to take a loss at any time. I think it's more trying to get beaten the first game of the season, at home and in front of our friends and families than at any other time. However, it's done and over and the sooner forgotten the better.

"It's a poor time to rehash the unpleasantness we witnessed this afternoon on the field. That happened in our own house, so to speak, before thirty thousand people who turned out to see a clean, hard game of football. In all my years of coaching, I have never seen such a disgraceful display of poor sportsmanship, lack of emotional control, unrestrained actions, and contemptible disregard for the spirit of the game. The players who took part have been dismissed from the squad.

"Now, back to something a little more pleasant. One defeat does not make a season, and I never felt it did anyone any good to look over his shoulder and try to count his mistakes. I, for one, am looking ahead to the conference championship. I hope you are too. A victory over Brandon next Saturday will be the first big step."

After Ralston and Rockwell left, Chip dressed slowly and then rode to Grayson's with Soapy and Fireball in the Finley VW. It was a long evening. Skip tried to cheer him up, but the teenager's attempts merely added to Chip's gloom. Skip had sat with his uncle and Coach Carpenter at the game.

"Uncle Merton was almost as mad as I was after the fumble," Skip confided. "It's a good thing he didn't run into Mr. Jacobs or Mr. Aker at the game. He sure would have told them off. He said the touchdown twins come by their meanness legitimately enough; they're just like their fathers when it comes to poor sportsmanship."

University High School's football stadium was jammed with spectators that Friday night. Chip was squeezed between Skip's uncle and Sam Riggs, the corporate pilot for Blaine Technology. They were seated on the fifty-yard line right behind the University High School bench.

University's marching band and majorettes were parading down the center of the field, led by baton twirlers, while the visitors' band was lined up behind the goal at the other end of the field. As the cheerleaders entertained the crowd on each side of the field, the players of both teams were warming up in front of their benches. Although it was not yet dark, the lights had been turned on and added to the colorful, energetic scene.

"Isn't it unusual for you and Skip to both be off on the same evening?" Blaine asked.

"Skip and I have been putting in extra time," Chip explained. "Besides, Mr. Grayson has extra weekend help."

"Grayson must be a football fan."

Chip smiled. "He sure is. He likes all sports."

"I can't understand why Skip wanted that job," Blaine mused, half to himself and half aloud. He turned and eyed Chip curiously. "Or you either," he said, "come to think of it. Don't you have an athletic scholarship? Doesn't it take care of all your school expenses?"

"No, I'm not at State on a scholarship, Mr. Blaine."

"You mean they didn't give you a scholarship? The way you play football? You must have had offers to go to other schools."

"Yes, I had other offers; but my dad played here, and State was where I always wanted to go to school. They offered me a scholarship, but I prefer to work."

"What in the world for?"

Chip thought a moment before replying. Then he spoke slowly and carefully. "Well, I guess I wanted to pay my own way. And I can play or not play and no one can complain."

"Don't you like football?"

"Oh, sure! I like a lot of things about football . . . like the excitement and thrills of playing and being with the guys and being part of a team."

"You could have all that and not have to work. I don't get it." He leaned forward and addressed his pilot. "What do you think about it, Riggs?"

"Oh," the pilot said slowly, "I don't know much about football. I suppose there's a sort of prestige that goes with an athlete getting a scholarship for playing the game. It means he's considered something special, I guess."

"What's wrong with that?" Blaine persisted.

"Well," the pilot continued thoughtfully, "I guess football is to Hilton what flying is to me. I fly because I love it. I guess Hilton plays football for the sheer love of the game."

"What's that got to do with working?"

"Nothing," Riggs said. He thought a moment and then continued. "Maybe Hilton likes to feel that he's playing football on his own. You know, for the love of the game. Frankly, if I could afford a plane, I don't think I would work at flying."

Chip listened to Riggs in admiration. The pilot's feelings about flying were the same as his own for football.

"Well," Blaine concluded, "Skip won't have to worry about working or anything like that. He's got a scholarship for four straight years at Brand. Housing, meals, tuition, books, fees—the works."

"I know," Chip said. "I saw it."

"You saw it?"

Chip nodded. "Yes, sir. Skip showed me the letter of intent."

Blaine grinned. "I guess that's the reason he hasn't given it back. He must be showing it to everyone in town."

The pregame activities on the field were finished, and the teams had circled in front of their benches. The cheerleaders for both teams alternated in leading cheers before the officials gathered in a little knot in the middle of the field. Chip felt a glow of pride when Skip dashed out from the University bench. The appearance of the all-state star set off a crowd cheer that was deafening. There was no question how the fans felt about Coleman Merton "Skip" Miller.

The crowd quieted while the officials were meeting with the captains. Two men sitting directly in front of Mr. Blaine began talking about Skip. "He looks like Hilton," one man said, "like State's all-American quarterback."

"He couldn't carry Hilton's shoes," the other said disdainfully.

"Well, he can carry *one* of them! And the way he's developing, he'll be able to carry 'em both in another year or so."

Blaine grinned and elbowed Chip. He was enjoying the conversation and leaned forward so he wouldn't miss any of it. Chip was embarrassed, but he couldn't do anything about it.

"Wonder what this kid is going to do about college? I heard that more than a hundred schools have contacted him."

The first speaker snickered. "It doesn't mean a thing. I hear some relative wants him to go to a college on the West Coast."

"So what?"

"So he goes to the college on the West Coast."

"What's a relative got to do with it?"

"He's some big business guy. You know that new technology firm just outside University? Well, he just about owns it."

"So?"

"So the kid's father works for him, and what the uncle tells the father to do, he does. Probably the kid too!"

"Maybe you're right," the other agreed. "But it seems a shame the kid can't go to college right here where he grew up, where everyone knows him and all—"

The roar of the crowd burst forth again when the teams ran out on the field for the opening kickoff, interrupting the conversation. Chip breathed a sigh of relief. He was feeling a little uncomfortable just being with E. Merton Blaine without having to listen to a couple of fans talk about him too. He was glad he was leaving early to get ready for the team's trip to Brandon.

The high school teams were lined up, and Skip was standing in front of the University goal line, a little ahead of the position Chip always took. He looked at the University bench and found Coach Carpenter standing on the sideline, anxiously watching his team.

Then the ball was in the air. It was a short kick and didn't reach Skip. That was the only reason he wasn't in the play. After the ball was down and as soon as the University team was positioned on the thirty-yard line, he personally took charge. He carried for ten yards on a keeper, passed to his left end for eight, carried again for six, and passed to his right end for fifteen. The steam-rolling would have continued for a touchdown if the opponents' captain hadn't called a time-out, suddenly realizing the ball was on his own thirty-one-yard line.

The time-out didn't change anything. Skip took up right where he had left off. The game was only six minutes old when University scored the first touchdown, and Skip kicked for the extra point. The opponents received but couldn't gain and had to punt. Then Skip started all over again. That's the way the game went. It was all

University High, and the half ended with the local team leading 21-0.

When it was time for Chip to leave, he thanked Mr. Blaine and shook hands warmly with Sam Riggs. He wouldn't forget the pilot for a long time. And that night, before the humming of the bus wheels lulled him to sleep, he thought of Riggs's philosophy. He surmised there could be people all over who viewed life like that. If only he could have a chance to know them.

CHAPTER 16

Sophomore Spoilers

BRANDON STADIUM was almost filled when the University Statesmen ran out on the field. And by the time they had finished warming up, every seat in the open air stadium was taken. Coach Ralston and Murph Kelly watched every move Ace Gibbons made. Chip could tell they were deeply concerned about Ace's knee.

Chip won the toss and chose to receive. The ball went to Speed on the kickoff, and the fleet halfback carried to midfield, nearly breaking into the open for a touchdown. But he was hit hard, and Chip noticed his friend was limping when he got up. Chip pulled one of Speed's arms over his shoulder and tried to help the speedster walk it off.

"It feels pretty bad, Chip," Speed panted. He winced and shook his head. "Man, I don't think I can run on it."

Chip motioned toward the bench, and Ralston sent Junior Roberts in to replace Speed. On the first play from scrimmage, Chip surprised the Brandon secondary when he hit Montague on a long pass at the Brandon ten-yard line. The slender end scored standing up.

Brandon came right back to score, and the teams alternated touchdowns once more. It was 14-14 at the half, and 16-14 in favor of Brandon at the end of the third quarter.

In the fourth quarter Ace Gibbons intercepted a Brandon pass, and a key block made it possible for him to go all the way for the touchdown. Ace's run had been beautiful to watch but very costly. His knee had been hurt again, and Murph Kelly took him out of the game.

Coach Ralston sent Bob Horton in to replace Ace, and Chip kicked the extra point to make the score State 21, Brandon 16.

The Statesmen's fighting defense, backed up by Chip's kicking, held Brandon in their own territory for the rest of the game. The final score: State 21, Brandon 16.

It was a happy squad that piled on the State University team bus for the ride back to University the next morning. The Statesmen had won their first conference game, and the players were looking ahead to the rest of the games, discussing the strong and the weak teams in the conference.

Chip wasn't engaging in that talk. Every game and every team were tough. He was thinking about Ace and Speed. Murph Kelly had said Speed's ankle was sprained, and Ace's knee was about as bad.

"Seven more to go," he murmured, shaking his head worriedly. Without Whitty and the touchdown twins, the future was far from bright.

When the bus reached University on Sunday morning, the parking lot at Assembly Hall was crowded with friends and fans. Chip and Soapy helped Speed down the steps, and the first person they saw was Skip. Whittemore was right behind him. Skip rushed forward and grabbed their bags. "Welcome home! Nice going! Nice run, Ace! Tough luck, Speed. Follow me, guys!"

The high school senior led the way and nodded toward a shiny red convertible parked at the curb. "Not bad, huh?"

"Wow!" Soapy said. "What a machine!"

"Get in," Skip said. "I'll drive you over to Jeff."

"Wow, your old man must have some big bucks," Soapy exclaimed.

"It isn't his," Skip said. "The car belongs to Uncle Merton."

"I thought so," Chip said quietly. His eyes searched Skip's face. "The first thing you know, you'll be so obligated to your uncle that you'll *have* to go to Brand."

"No, I won't."

"What about the letter, Skip?"

"I haven't signed it and I'm not going to."

"Well," Soapy said impatiently, "let's get this baby rolling."

Whittemore sat beside Skip in the front seat, and Chip and Soapy flanked Speed in the back as the sleek car rolled smoothly away. Whittemore passed a copy of the *Herald* back to Chip. "Look at the headline!" he said.

"Oh, no," Chip said shortly.

STATE'S ALL-AMERICAN STARS
AS FIREBRANDS BOW, 21-16

Chip Hilton hit Chris Montague with a scoring pass on the first scrimmage play of the game here today and sprung the Statesmen to a 21-16 triumph over Brandon before a Firebrand Stadium throng of 32,290.

The Hilton-Montague passing combination enabled the Statesmen to match Brandon's two touchdowns until the second half, when the Firebrands went two points ahead on a safety. Then Gibbons brought the Statesmen from behind with a pass interception on the State 32-yard line. His 68-yard touchdown gallop iced the bitter struggle.

"Now, look at Bill Bell's column," Whitty directed.

"I'll read it out loud," Soapy volunteered. "Hey, listen to this!"

"As I predicted yesterday, State's much-publicized touchdown twins, Travis Aker and Jack Jacobs, did not make the trip to Brandon. Coach Curly Ralston is disciplining the Sorry Sophomore Spoilers for their part in the unsportsmanlike skirmish during the Templeton game. Judging from their performance in the Templeton game and the ease with which they committed so many disastrous mistakes, it's probably a good thing they were left behind."

Soapy paused and added a solemn "Amen" before he continued.

"Ralston subbed infrequently and was back with his veterans yesterday. We all expected a great deal out of State this year, but Ralston's team will be lucky to squeak through the season without a few more injuries. Unfortunately, that means a few more defeats despite the brilliance of Chip Hilton and State's great forward line.

"In fact, senior Ace Gibbons is already handicapped with a sprained knee that forced him to the sideline in the last quarter of the Brandon game, and the talented Speed Morris is nursing a sprained ankle that will sideline him for at least a week or more. . . ."

Chip reached over and took the paper out of Soapy's hands. Then, to the amazement of his companions, he said, "*That's* why we need Aker and Jacobs."

Skip's hands jumped on the wheel, and he nearly ran the car up on the curb. "*Need* them?" he echoed. "Are you serious?"

"I've never been more serious in my life," Chip said grimly. "And I intend to get them back. Whitty too—"

"Man, Chip," Soapy protested, "come off it! Aker and Jacobs just aren't worth it. Whitty, yes. Aker and Jacobs, no."

"Amen," Speed said, imitating Soapy.

"It's got to be all three or none," Chip argued.

"You're wasting your time," Whittemore said, shaking his head.

"Not if you're willing to help."

"What can I do?" Whittemore asked, shrugging his shoulders.

"Apologize to Jacobs."

The big end twisted his torso around and leaned over the seat. He looked at Chip in astonishment. "You mean you want *me* to apologize?"

"That's right," Chip stated, eyeing Whitty evenly.

"You're kidding. Why should *I* apologize?"

"You started the trouble. You hit him first."

"But I saw him deliberately grab the ball."

"Yes," Chip agreed, "but that didn't give you the right to hit him."

Whittemore shook his head. "I still don't get it."

"You want to play football, don't you? And you want to help the team, right?"

Whittemore nodded. "Of course I do, Chip."

"All right then. You can make a big step toward getting back on the team by apologizing to Jacobs."

"How about Aker? How about him apologizing to *me?* He hit me first." Whittemore rubbed his mouth gently. "And last!" he added grimly.

"I think he *will* apologize to you if you talk to Jacobs."

Whittemore scratched his head and thought it over. "Tell you what," he said thoughtfully. "I'll let you know in a couple of days. OK?"

Skip pulled up in front of Jefferson Hall with a flourish. Chip and Soapy helped Speed up to his room, thanking Skip for the ride. The three friends spent the rest of the day studying for tests and working on papers for their classes.

Whittemore's "couple of days" lasted all week. Chip mentioned it once or twice, but the big end put him off.

The big game with Eastern was the talk of the campus, town, and Grayson's. Chip was kept busy with Ralston's new plays and defensive plans for the game and didn't notice the level of excitement in University about the upcoming game.

The *Herald* and the *News* played up the Eastern players and the national title ambitions of the visitors every day, but Chip and the rest of the veterans weren't impressed. Eastern was an independent team, and a victory or a loss meant nothing to State in the conference standings. So Chip and the majority of his teammates were looking forward to the game. They felt it was a great opportunity for State to upset the favorite.

Coach Ralston spent a lot of time with Eddie Anderson and Bob Horton during the week, giving them extra tutoring as halfbacks. But neither showed much promise, and it was obvious to the rest of the squad that Chip and Fireball would have to carry the burden of the offense all alone.

Chip practiced his passing with Red and Monty every evening. But neither could come close to replacing Whitty. Red wasn't as big and he didn't have the hands or the pass-receiving know-how. Monty was tall and fast, but his blocking was inconsistent. He was so slender that Chip winced every time the skinny sophomore was tackled or tried to throw a block.

Saturday dawned clear and cold with only a slight breeze when the State University team took to the field to warm up. Chip started slowly with his kicking. He watched the Eastern kicker punting on the opposite side of the field, figuring the distance and height of his opponent's punts. Soon they were matching booming punts.

While he was kicking, he was thinking ahead to the game. Ace was going to start, but Chip didn't think the hurt player would be much help. Ace's knee was bandaged until it seemed nearly the size of a pillow.

I'll try to do a lot of passing and running myself, Chip thought. *That'll help take the pressure off him.*

Asking to be on the receiving unit, Chip got his chance on the opening kickoff. He won the toss and chose to receive. The ball came straight to him on the State goal line. He headed upfield and made it to the twenty-five-yard line before he was gang-tackled and buried under a pile of bulky bodies.

The piling seemed a little too vicious to Chip. The penalty flag flew into the air as the official agreed. After he had pulled the reluctant Eastern players off the pile, the official glanced sharply at Chip and then picked up the ball and stepped off fifteen yards.

"Personal foul—late hit by the defense—fifteen yards," he announced. When the Eastern captain protested, the same official growled, "Play football!"

Chip followed his plan, alternating his running and passing, and State moved to the Eastern twenty-seven-yard line before the drive was checked. Then, on fourth down, Chip booted a three-pointer. State was out in front!

Those three points looked big during the first half. But the Statesmen were outmanned, and the visitors pushed them down the field again and again. Eastern seemed to be knocking at the State door the entire thirty minutes. Chip ran and passed when he could, and his long, perfectly placed punts held the opponents in check. The score at the end of the half: State 3, Eastern 0.

Eastern continued the same tactics in the second half. They confined their attack to the ground, substituted their players in and out with ease, and kept the Statesmen on the defense.

Eddie Anderson was trying but lacked confidence, and Ace couldn't run fast enough to do any good. It was Fireball on the short inside plunges and Chip on the off-tackle slants and outside sprints that kept State in the ball game. Eastern would drive to the State twenty and then run into a fighting defense that refused to give an inch.

Every State fan in the stadium was on their feet as the game drew to a close, giving their team thundering support. An undermanned State University team was holding one of the football powers of the nation at bay. No! Beating them! Leading in the score! Now *this* was a team!

With ten seconds to play, the ball on the State thirty-yard line, third down and seven to go, Eastern took a time-out to make one final assault on the State goal line. Ralston hadn't made a substitution in this series but had relented when Chip asked to play in the defensive secondary.

Chip studied the dirty, sweat-soaked uniforms and drawn, tired faces of his teammates, and his heart swelled with pride. Ace was a battered wreck of a man, barely able to move. Monty was exhausted but still ready to fight. Eddie Anderson was ready to drop. Chip looked at the clock. Ten seconds. If they could only hold them once more . . . .

An entire Eastern platoon of fresh substitutes came racing in: uniforms new, shiny, clean, and dry; confident in action and manner; spirits high.

"Only ten more seconds, guys," Chip urged. "Just one more play."

Time was in now, and Eastern came charging out of their huddle and formed in the same tight, power-packed formation. The play started off like a sweep, but it was a fake, and the quarterback faded back for a pass. Two receivers were splitting Ace in his defensive right-linebacker position, and Eastern's halfback was sprinting toward Chip.

Chip saw the play coming. The Eastern quarterback had known about Ace's knee all along!

It was a reckless move, but Chip left his position and sprinted to help Ace. But even as he raced toward the fighting linebacker, Chip knew it was too late. The visitors' quarterback dug in and fired a perfect peg to the outside receiver. The Eastern end caught the ball without breaking stride. The other receiver took Ace out an instant later with a hard block, and the ball carrier crossed the goal ten feet ahead of Chip.

Touchdown!

Chip hurried back to help Ace to his feet, but the veteran player couldn't make it. He rested painfully on his good knee, shaking his head in remorse. "I'm sorry about the pass, Chip," he said. "My knee just seemed to give out."

Murph Kelly came in with two of his assistants, and they put Ace's arms over their shoulders and led him from the field. Junior Roberts reported for Ace, and the teams formed for the extra-point attempt. The Eastern kicker booted a perfect placement and the game was over, Eastern 7, State 3.

Most of the visiting scouts had taken copious notes covering the offensive and defensive formations used by the Statesmen. But the keen-eyed A & M scout had written only a few significant sentences. "Really only eleven solid players on each side of the line. No reserves to speak of. Injuries. A triple-threat quarterback who can do everything but who has only a fullback to run the ball and no pass receivers. Number 22, bad leg—flood his zone with passes. Make State play a sixty-minute game; tire them out."

CHAPTER 17

Playing with Heart

PHILIP WHITTEMORE glanced at Skip and tossed the sports page of the *Herald* on the desk. "Did you see what Bill Bell said about the team?"

"I saw it," Skip said quickly. "He said State was a team with a lot of handicaps but also a team with a lot of heart."

"That's right," Whittemore said seriously. "It made me think about what you said, Chip—how I was part of the problem. When can we go see Jack Jacobs?"

Chip was hoisting a box of supplies onto the top shelf, and Whitty's words caught him by surprise, but only for a second. He whirled around to face his friend. "You mean it, Whitty?"

"I sure do!" Whittemore said firmly. "The sooner the better."

"I know where they hang," Skip said eagerly. "They'll be in their dorm rooms or at The Prospector. Want me to see if they're there?"

Chip thought about it for a few seconds. "That restaurant is only a few minutes from here," he said tentatively.

"I'll be right back," Skip said, dashing for the door.

It seemed as if he had been gone only two minutes before he was back, breathing rapidly. "They're there!" he said breathlessly. "Just the two of them. Studying! In the last booth on the right."

"Let's go!" Whittemore said shortly.

There were only a few customers in the restaurant. Just as Skip had said, Travis Aker and Jack Jacobs had taken command of the last booth, their books and papers spread out on the table.

When Chip and Whitty stopped beside the booth, Travis Aker looked up in surprise. His expression changed instantly to wariness as he nudged Jacobs. "Look who's here! Surprise, surprise!"

"Mind if we sit down?" Chip asked.

"Mind?" Jacobs said elaborately. "Why, we're delighted!" He winked at Aker and waved toward the other side of the table. "Sit down. Imagine meeting the famous all-American passing combination *face to face.*"

"We've met before," Chip said calmly.

"What's on your mind?" Jacobs asked, looking at Whittemore.

"Something you probably don't expect," Whittemore said. "Anyway, I'm here to apologize for starting the trouble on the field. I'm sorry. Is that good enough?"

Jacobs's eyes widened, and he stared at Whittemore in surprise. "I guess so," he managed. "What's with you?"

"I don't suppose you read Bill Bell's column today, did you?"

Jacobs shook his head. "I never read his column. So? What was so important about it?"

Whittemore pulled the clipping from his pocket and smoothed it out on the table between Jacobs and Aker. "Read it," he said quietly.

Jacobs and Aker read the article clear through to the end. Then Aker looked up and smiled. "I get it," he said, grinning maliciously. "You want to patch things up and then go crawling back to Ralston and tell him you apologized and you're sorry and see if he'll put you back on the team. Right?"

"Sure!" Jacobs said. "That's it! Good ol' Hilton needs his favorite pass receiver."

"The *team* needs him," Chip said gently. "And the team needs you guys. Badly."

"Yeah, right!" Aker said bitterly. "Sure the team needs us. Now that your buddies are hurt."

"Did Ralston send you?" Jacobs asked.

Chip shook his head. "No one sent us. Whitty and I figured if we could get the trouble with you guys straightened out, the coach might forget about it."

"We're not interested," Aker said coldly. "We're going to transfer out of State. Dad and Jack's father are trying to get us into Brand. They know the head of the booster club."

"That's right," Jacobs added. "We couldn't care less about Ralston or State or—"

"Or you two guys," Aker added. "Wait!" he said quickly. "I'll take that back. I guess *you're* all right, Whittemore. It's the rest of that bunch. I'm sorry I hit you, Whittemore."

"Me, too," Whittemore replied. "I'm glad we talked, for what it's worth."

"I guess you understand the NCAA transfer rule," Chip said quietly. "You'll have to sit out a year and lose a whole season of football."

"So what! We're thinkin' about petitioning the NCAA to let us play without waiting a year," Jacobs said carelessly, shrugging his shoulders.

Chip felt they had made progress and didn't want to push their luck. If he could bring the team into line, he would be in a good position to approach Coach Ralston. "Well," he said, rising from the table, "I have to get back to work. Sorry you guys can't see how much this would help the team. Let's go, Whitty."

As the two friends left The Prospector, Whitty turned and said, "Thanks, Chip. You were right. I'm glad we went to talk to Aker and Jacobs. I feel better since I cleared the air and apologized. But it doesn't sound like they'll come back to the team."

Chip nodded. "I think you did the right thing, Whitty. Maybe they'll still come around."

Skip was waiting when they got back. "What happened?" he asked.

Whitty told him about the conversation while he was putting on his fountain uniform, white slacks and a colorful red and blue polo shirt. "So," he concluded, "we had a nice walk."

"I know one thing," Skip said. "They won't get very far with Uncle Merton on the booster club. He thinks they're the world's worst."

Chip hoped that Skip was right. But no matter what Aker and Jacobs thought, he wasn't going to give up.

Coach Ralston called off all scrimmage practices for the week, giving his tired and injured regulars a rest. Ace and Speed managed to get loosened up by Friday afternoon, and when the Statesmen left for Southwestern that night, they had high hopes that their two injured stars would be all right for the second conference game of the season.

But the next afternoon Ace lasted only one play. Chip won the toss and chose to receive. The kick went to Fireball, who carried to the thirty-one-yard line.

Ace hobbled into the huddle, his face drawn with pain. "It's hurt again," he groaned. "Sorry, guys, I can't do you any good."

Junior Roberts replaced him. Once again, Chip found himself in the middle of a game with only Fireball to depend on for ball-carrying help.

Southwestern stressed defense, and when the Statesmen failed to penetrate beyond the Southwestern twenty-yard line, Chip kicked a field goal for three points. The home team received and marched the length of the field, using a spread formation for short passes and end runs to score. From State's vantage point, the only positive of Southwestern's drive was the missed extra point. Chip kicked another field goal in the second quarter, and the score was tied at 6-6 when the half ended.

To open the second half, Southwestern received, couldn't gain, and kicked to the University Statesmen on the State thirty-five-yard line. On the very first play, Roberts was hit hard and fumbled. Southwestern recovered it. Thirty seconds later, the Southwestern quarterback passed to his left end. The State second-string defender wasn't big enough to knock the ball away. The tall end pulled it in easily and carried to the nineteen-yard line. Three plays later they went around their left end for a touchdown. This time they kicked the extra point to take the lead, 13-6.

The teams seesawed back and forth in the last quarter until there were only three minutes left to play. Chip's kicking had forced Southwestern back again and again. Now, State took a low punt from a stalled Southwestern drive and raced back to the home team's thirty-three-yard line.

Chip hit Montague with a short pass, carried once himself to the eight-yard line on a keeper play, and hit Montague in the end zone for a touchdown. The cheering was loud and long for the visiting team's effort.

Southwestern now led by a single point, 13-12, and Chip faced a difficult decision. A successful placekick would tie the score; a successful running play or pass would win the game. And a failure on either play meant defeat.

Chip looked at his teammates' tired faces and grinned confidently. "We'll go for the two points! OK? All right! Keeper 9 X! On two! Let's win! Break!"

The Southwestern fans were chanting, "Block that kick! Block that kick!" But when State broke for the line and stood in scrimmage formation, they changed it to "Hold that line! Hold that line!"

Chip faked to Fireball and then to Roberts before he tore around right end with Soapy leading the way. The redhead dropped the outside linebacker, and Chip ran clear to the sideline before he cut in and plunged across the goal line for the two points.

The chant of the Southwestern home fans ended in a groan as the referee raised his hands and the big numbers under the clock showed the score: Visitors 14, Southwestern 13.

There was time for one more play. Southwestern received as Chip booted a high kick. The ball carried to Southwestern's thirty-yard line. Biggie, Soapy, and Red hit the fullback an instant after he caught the ball. The game was over! State had bounced back into the winning column.

When the team arrived in University, the parking lot was again crowded with students and fans. Skip met Chip and Soapy just as he had after the Brandon game. But this time, to Soapy's disappointment, Skip wasn't driving the convertible.

"Where's the dream machine?" Soapy demanded.

"I'm not driving it anymore," Skip said.

"But how will my fans recognize me?" Soapy asked mournfully. "Why not?"

"I don't want to obligate myself," Skip said, winking at Chip. "Hey! Nice win, you guys. We won too!"

"Chip won it for us," Soapy said proudly.

"The papers say the same thing," Skip said, grinning. "This week the headline reads: 'Hilton Upsets Unbeaten Southwestern!'"

"Of all the nonsense—" Chip began.

"And," Skip interrupted, "Western beat A & M!"

"No!" Soapy exploded.

"That's right!"

"Well, whaddaya know," Soapy said, his eyes wide. He counted on his fingers. "Now all we gotta do is beat Cathedral, Southern, Midwestern, Western, and A & M! Man, that's a cinch! A & M beat Cathedral 31-6; we'll take Southern easy. Midwestern and Western are tough, all right, but we'll kill A & M—"

"If you don't run out of healthy players," Skip added.

"Let's just concentrate on Cathedral," Chip said tiredly, "and win—"

"I know, I know," Soapy interrupted happily, "and win 'em one at a time."

Cathedral fielded a fighting team, and what had figured to be an easy victory turned into a bitter battle. Playing without Ace or Speed, State scored first, chiefly through Fireball's inside plunging and Chip's dashes off-tackle and around the ends. Chip kicked the try for the extra point. The visitors came right back, took the kickoff, and marched the length of the field to score and kick the extra point. Chip kicked two field goals in the second quarter, and State led 13-7 at the half.

The visitors moved ahead in the third quarter to lead 15-13. With time running out in the last quarter, Chip faded back to pass, but Cathedral had Montague completely covered. Chip hit Fireball instead, with a pass over the line following a fake plunge. The speedy blockbuster sprinted thirty yards for the touchdown. That put State out in front, 19-15. After the touchdown, Chip fooled Cathedral with a fake placekick and passed to Red in the end zone for the two points. The final score: State 21, Cathedral 15.

The victory ran State's conference record to three wins and no defeats, but the problem of the starting halfback positions on the offense and key linebacker spots on the defense were cause for alarm and dampened the team's enthusiasm.

Coach Ralston worked feverishly all week, but little progress seemed to have been made when the team left Friday afternoon for the game with Southern.

That game developed into another dogfight. The home team was big and determined and scored twice in the first half, leading State 14 to 7 at halftime. In the third quarter Southern kicked a short field goal to lead 17-7, but State came right back with a long run by Chip and a thirty-yard pass to Fireball for the touchdown. Chip passed to Montague for the extra two points. That made the score Southern 17, State 15.

After several punt exchanges toward the end of the fourth quarter, State wound up with the ball on the Southern thirty-two-yard line. It was fourth down, four to go, and only enough time for one more play. Coach Ralston called Chip to the sideline for their final time-out. He talked with the offensive line briefly and then decided to go for a field goal to win the game.

With the deafening crowd roar rolling down on the field in a wave, Chip toed the most important kick of the game. With back-up quarterback Gary Young holding, Chip's kick split the uprights for three points. The final score: State 18, Southern 17.

The battle-weary Statesmen could hardly walk, but they weren't too tired to get Chip on their shoulders and carry him all the way to the locker room. "Four straight conference wins!" Soapy shouted gleefully. "And only three to go!"

CHAPTER 18

Playing in the Grandstand

CHIP AND SOAPY were reading the Sunday papers when someone bellowed the announcement from Jeff's first floor. "Chip Hilton! Chip, there's someone out front to see you."

"I wonder who that could be," Chip muttered. He walked over to the door. "Coming!" he called. "I'm coming right down."

Soapy bounded to the window to look down at the street. "It's that cool convertible Skip was driving," he said excitedly. "The top's down and everything! There's a big man sitting in the back seat smoking a cigar. It must be Skip's uncle."

"I hope not," Chip said earnestly, pulling a bright red State sweatshirt over his head. "I wonder what's up?"

A man in a chauffeur's uniform was waiting on the porch. "Chip Hilton?" he asked. Without waiting for Chip's reply, he gestured toward the street. "Mr. Blaine would like to speak to you."

Blaine took a last puff from his cigar and tossed it on the

street when Chip approached. "Hello, Hilton. Glad you were at the dorm. How about a little drive?"

"All right, Mr. Blaine," Chip said reluctantly.

The chauffeur held the car door open, and Chip sat down beside Mr. Blaine. As the convertible rolled smoothly away, Chip glanced up at the window of his room on the second floor. Soapy was leaning far out the window, clowning around and waving good-bye.

"Oh, before I forget," Mr. Blaine said. "How did you make out with the touchdown twins?"

Chip glanced at the big man in surprise. "How did—"

Blaine smiled. "Skip keeps me pretty well advised about your team activities."

Chip shook his head ruefully. "I'm not doing too well, I guess."

"From what Skip said, they were counting on transferring to Brand."

"I know," Chip said, nodding.

"Well," Blaine continued, "the two boys and their fathers paid me a little visit a day or two ago. They had a few misconceptions concerning the NCAA guidelines for transferring athletes. They obviously don't understand the Brand coaching staff, and they were all mixed up about the caliber and quality of athletes Brand is interested in. I think I straightened them out on all counts.

"We wouldn't have them on a Brand team. They wouldn't last five minutes with Stew Peterson, and unless I'm greatly mistaken, they're not worth five minutes of *your* time."

"They've got a lot of ability," Chip said tentatively.

"Physically, yes," Blaine agreed. "But when it comes to guts, determination, and a knowledge of team play, they haven't got a thing. And their fathers are just as bad. I told them so."

"But we haven't got much depth at those key positions, Mr. Blaine," Chip said.

"I know," Blaine replied sympathetically. "I don't know where in the world you men mustered enough depth to win any games, much less four."

He appraised Chip and continued. "From the look of you, I would say that right now you need a long rest. I think Ralston is playing you too much. When a player gets tired and worn out, he goes stale, and that's when injuries occur."

"There isn't much Coach Ralston can do about that," Chip said apologetically. "We're all playing lots of minutes. All the veterans, that is."

Blaine nodded. "I know. But I'm getting away from the purpose of this little ride. I wanted to talk to you about Skip."

"About going to college?"

"That's right. The boy has gained a lot of confidence and independence since he got that job with you. He doesn't want to use my car and won't commit himself to Brand."

Blaine paused and studied Chip before continuing. "Skip tells me you think he should go to State."

"I guess that's right," Chip said honestly, nodding. "My father went to State, Mr. Blaine. But that isn't the only reason I came to school here. I was born in this state, and I have always felt an athlete owed something to his home state. I'm for State first, last, and all the time."

There was a short, awkward pause as the powerful car moved swiftly along the open highway. "You know, Hilton," Mr. Blaine said, "Skip's father has had a rather tough time of it in life. Besides, he's an independent sort of a fellow. Now, when Skip needs his financial help, he is in no position to contribute much. In fact, he needs Skip's help."

"I thought Mr. Miller was working for you."

Blaine smiled. "Well, let's say he's working in one of my plants. In fact, the job he holds right now is a *made* job."

Chip wished he had never come on this ride. *Why in the world did I ever let myself get involved in Skip's problem?*

"You could help Skip a lot," Blaine continued. "His father knows he could really *earn* his pay in my western plant. He would go in a second if Skip went along."

"You want me to advise Skip to go to Brand," Chip said quietly. "Isn't that right?"

"That's right," Blaine said. "I'm sure it's best for everyone."

"I'm sorry, Mr. Blaine," Chip said firmly. "I can't do that." He faced the big man and looked him straight in the eyes. "I still think Skip should go to State. However, I assure you that I won't try to influence him. Skip should make his own decisions. If you don't mind, I'd like to go back to the dorm."

"Sure, Hilton," Blaine said kindly. "We'll go back. I hope you won't say anything about this afternoon to Skip."

"I won't, Mr. Blaine."

The drive back to Jefferson Hall was quiet and swift, and Chip was glad when the car glided gently to a stop in front of his dorm. He thanked Mr. Blaine for the ride and got out of the car quickly, glad the ordeal was over and anxious to get back to his books.

Soapy had gone out somewhere. Chip spent the rest of the afternoon studying, but once in a while he took a short break to think about Aker and Jacobs. Now that Mr. Blaine had set them straight about transferring to Brand, maybe they would be more receptive to his plan. "I'll talk to them first thing in the morning," he resolved.

His Monday schedule was light, and Chip usually spent a lot of time studying in the library. He had his own study cubicle on the tenth floor of Metcalf Library, overlooking Assembly Hall and the football fields beyond. But today he broke his routine and tramped around campus, looking for Aker and Jacobs. It was nearly noon before he caught up with them in the Student Union. They were sitting alone in one of the lounges, their science books piled on a table.

"Hey, guys," he said, dropping down into a chair beside them. "I've been looking for you. How's it going?"

"Better than it is with you," Jacobs said seriously. He looked at Travis, and they both nodded. "You look awful. You must have lost fifteen pounds."

"Not quite," Chip said, smiling because the two wanted to talk. "But I *am* a little tired."

"You ought to be," Aker said. "Seems Ralston's been playing you every minute of the games."

"There isn't much else he can do, Travis. That's why I'm here."

"I thought so," Jacobs said quickly. "Don't you ever give up?"

"Nope, I don't." Chip grinned tiredly before setting his jaw.

"You might as well," Aker said. "We're not going to cave in just to help Ralston out of a hole he dug himself."

"I'm not thinking about the coach," Chip said evenly. "It's for the team. We need help."

"You don't need us," Aker said bitterly. "We've run into Gibbons and Brennan and some of the rest of them a dozen times, and they treat us like we're dirt."

"And they've got half the campus acting the same way," Jacobs added.

"What do you expect?" Chip asked. "They think you quit."

"We didn't quit," Jacobs said sullenly. "Ralston *threw* us off the team. What would *you* do?"

"I would try to get back on the team," Chip said simply. "I'd find a way to show the coaches I really wanted to play football."

"Look, Hilton," Aker said, getting to his feet and gathering up his books, "we wanted to play football. That's why we came to State. But it wasn't any secret how Gibbons and Brennan and the rest of the starters felt about us. We got a little publicity, and they ganged up on us from the very first day of workouts at Camp Sundown. We had to fight back."

"Right!" Jacobs added. "Maybe we did get a little out of line, but we weren't going to bow down to them just because we were sophomores."

"We know we're not the greatest," Aker said. "But we know we're good enough to play varsity. And if those guys had been real guys, we would have shown them we could block and tackle as well as they could. But no," he said, turning away, "they wanted to get rid of us. So we'll do our playing in the grandstand."

The two sophomores gathered up their books and walked slowly away. Chip could scarcely conceal his jubilation. "They're coming around," he whispered to himself. "Now to line up the team."

He approached Soapy, Biggie, Speed, Red, and Fireball first and had no difficulty in gaining their support. Then, on Wednesday, just before practice, he called a meeting of the starters and told them about his plan to get Whitty, Aker, and Jacobs back on the squad.

"Whitty, yes!" Brennan said. "The other two, no way!"

"Right!" Joe Maxim agreed. "We want no part of *them.*"

"Let it ride until after the Midwestern game, Chip," Biggie advised.

"Let it ride, period!" Brennan growled. "We've made it this far. We don't need any help *now.*"

Mike Brennan's remark turned out to be the understatement of the year. Saturday's game proved that. Midwestern was a strong defensive team and had State well scouted. The Midwesterners were ready for Finley's strong inside plunges and Chip's quick off-tackle slants and end runs. Double-teaming Montague, they knocked down Chip's passes all through the first quarter.

In the second quarter, with the ball in the possession of the Statesmen on their own forty-five-yard line, second down and eight to go, Chip called for a delayed pass to Red.

He faked to Finley and then to Anderson. He dropped back for the throw, and it happened!

Midwestern's right tackle and end rushed him and knocked him to the ground just as he released the ball. It was a clean hit, but Chip was caught off balance and tried to break the fall with his right hand. He saw Red catch the ball just as his right hand hit the ground. Then the charging opponents fell heavily on top of him, and his right arm was doubled under and behind his back.

Chip felt a tremendous pull and wrench in his shoulder, and it hurt so badly that he couldn't stop yelling out in pain. One of the opponents grasped him under the right arm to help him to his feet, but Chip pushed him away with his good left arm. "Hold it," he said loudly. Getting slowly to his feet, he winced at the pain. His right arm hung loosely at his side. "Oh, no!" he cried.

Red had been tackled on the Midwestern thirty-two-yard line, but he came tearing back to join the Statesmen gathered around Chip. The exultant shout with which the State fans had greeted Red's catch died away as Murph Kelly ran out on the field. And the stunned fans remained silent as Kelly led Chip from the field. All were shocked by the realization that the trainer had applied a hastily adjusted sling to the famous quarterback's throwing arm.

Curly Ralston and Henry Rockwell met them halfway to the bench, their faces etched with fear and concern. "How you feel, Chip? What is it, Murph? Is it bad?"

"It's bad," Kelly confirmed.

Dr. Mike Terring joined Chip and Murph as they moved along the sideline. The fans rose to their feet and applauded Chip all the way to the players' exit. When they reached the locker room, Dr. Terring waited quietly as Kelly cut the jersey and laces of the shoulder pads. Then, pressing gently on Chip's shoulder, he examined it carefully. At the end, he breathed a sigh of relief and nodded reassuringly at Chip.

"I can't find any signs of a break, Chip. Just the same, we'll go up to the medical center for an X ray. You get dressed and I'll be right back. I want to talk to the coaches."

"It doesn't feel so bad now, Doc. You don't think I should go back?"

"Back?" Terring repeated. "Of course not! You get dressed."

While Kelly helped him with his uniform, Chip tried to move his arm. But stiffness had set in, and a dull pain began coursing through his shoulder. "Just like Mr. Blaine said," he breathed. "I *was* tired." *Of all the times to get hurt!*

CHAPTER 19

The Name Is Chip

THE SPORTS PAGES of Sunday's *Herald* lying open on the hospital bed in the Medical Center told the story. Chip was sitting beside the window watching the driveway for Dr. Terring's car, and Soapy was sprawled on a chair in the corner staring glumly at the ceiling. The column's words kept racing through Chip's thoughts:

> State lost to Midwestern 7-0 for their first conference loss. Chip Hilton was hospitalized with a shoulder injury.

"Here he comes," Chip said, leaping to his feet.

A few moments later Dr. Terring tapped on the door and entered. He grinned at Soapy. "I figured you'd be here too." He turned to Chip. "Well, now, I expected to find *you* in bed."

"No, Doc, I'm all right. I feel fine. How about the X ray?"

Terring opened the envelope he was carrying and pulled out several prints. "Here they are, and there's not a sign of a break. Sit down on the side of the bed and let's have a look."

He took a long time examining Chip's shoulder, nodding now and then but saying nothing.

Soapy, shifting from one foot to the next, couldn't stand the suspense. "How about it? How's he doing, Doc?"

"So-so," Terring said.

"How about getting out of here?" Chip asked.

"I guess so," Terring said. "I can immobilize your shoulder by putting your arm in a sling."

"How soon can I go out to practice?" Chip asked. "How long before I can start throwing?"

Terring shook his head. "You're not going to do any more throwing this year, Chip. You might as well get that through your head now."

"But I can still play, Doc. I don't have to throw! We have an open date next Saturday. That means I've got two weeks—"

"You mean you'd play with one arm?"

"Sure, Doc. It's been done before."

"I know that," Terring said shortly, amazed at Chip's spirit. "Now, I want you to report to my office every afternoon. And until I tell you differently, you wear that sling. As soon as I can check you out of here, I'll drive you two back to the dorm."

When Terring dropped Chip and Soapy off at Jeff, all their friends were waiting in the lobby of the four-story brick residence hall. The reception warmed Chip's heart; all of them were trying to conceal their feelings by joking around, but underneath the lighthearted banter, he knew they were discouraged.

It was the same the next day on the campus. The Midwestern defeat had put the conference leadership in a three-way tie between State, A & M, and Western. Most State fans gave the injury-ridden Statesmen no chance for the conference title, especially with Chip on the disabled list.

Dr. Terring and Murph Kelly worked on his shoulder Monday afternoon, and Chip watched practice from the sidelines. Much of the pain had disappeared from his shoulder, but he could barely lift his arm, and he knew Mike Terring was right. He wasn't going to be able to throw for a long time.

At Grayson's, Skip was a tremendous help in the stockroom. He shouldered more responsibility so that Chip could spend most of his time at the desk. Skip and his teammates were undefeated, and the high school athlete should have been elated, but he was upset by his uncle's persistent campaign to send him to Brand University. His spirits were low, and he was unusually quiet.

It seemed to Chip that he was surrounded by trouble and discouragement, but none of it made sense. If Skip would only take a determined stand, his uncle would come around. Blood was a lot thicker than water and the happiness of a great nephew like Skip would certainly be more important to his uncle than the selection of a college just to play football.

As far as the Statesmen were concerned, they were still tied for first place in the conference. In fact, they were a game ahead because they had played five conference games while Western and A & M had only played four. And as he had witnessed time and again, anything could happen in football.

Tuesday afternoon, Chip saw Doc Terring early and waited in the locker room for the rest of his teammates. They were concerned about his shoulder, but he had no time for that. "Never mind me," he said. "I'll be all right. What about Aker and Jacobs? You said we should wait until after the Midwestern game." He smiled hopefully. "Well, it's after the Midwestern game."

There was an awkward silence. Then Mike Brennan cleared his throat and looked around at the others, as if for support. "How do we know they could help us, Chip? They never showed a thing."

"Maybe that was partly our fault," Chip said. "Or at least they feel that way."

"Naturally they would!" Ace Gibbons said.

"It doesn't seem to me," Biggie said slowly, "that we're in a position to debate their ability. Ace is out with a bum knee, Speed's ankle is no better, and Chip—"

"I'll be able to play," Chip interrupted. "Well, what do you say?"

"I say we let Chip try to get 'em back," Fireball said. "We sure know Whitty can help, and as far as Aker and Jacobs are concerned, what have we got to lose?"

"Nothing!" Soapy growled. "I'm game if they can help."

"They can help," Chip said. "But—"

"But what?" Brennan demanded.

"But isn't it important to think that we might help *them?* Help Aker and Jacobs? They were part of this team too. Wouldn't it be a good idea to forget the past and offer them a hand?"

"Nothing wrong with that in my book," Maxim agreed. There was a short silence.

Then Mike Brennan shrugged his broad shoulders. "All right, Chip. Count us in. You can tell 'em we'll start all over. Clean!"

It took Chip three days to find Aker and Jacobs. They were always a little ahead of him or had come along after he left. But on Friday he found them at lunch in the Student Union snack bar. Their attitudes surprised him.

"How's your shoulder?" Aker asked.

"It's coming along," Chip said, sitting down beside Jacobs. "Doc Terring says I can take the sling off this afternoon."

"You're going to try to play?" Jacobs asked curiously.

"I sure am!"

"But I read in the paper that you wouldn't be able to throw," Aker observed.

"True, but I can play without throwing. I was wondering about you guys—"

"You know where we stand," Jacobs said uncertainly. "What about the other guys on the team?"

"They feel exactly the same way I do," Chip said quickly.

"At least that's what they say," Aker said.

"How did you find *that* out?" Chip asked.

"Oh, we've still got a couple of friends on the team. They told us about the meeting you called last Tuesday and what you said."

"And about the one you had with them before the Midwestern game too," Jacobs added. "Look, I had you pegged all wrong, Chip. I'm sorry about that."

"That goes for both of us," Travis said. "Now, about coming back—we're out a year of football any way you look at it. We might as well play if Ralston will give us a chance."

"That's right," Jacobs agreed. "But we want to do something else! We want to show Ralston and the guys on the team that we're *real* football players."

"It appears to me we're forgetting something pretty important though," Aker said. "How about Ralston?"

"That's the next step," Chip said, rising to his feet. "Where can I reach you guys?"

"We live in Davis Hall," Jacobs said, grinning.

"We don't hang out there much, but we eat and study nearly every night at The Prospector," Aker added.

"Maybe we can change that to the training table," Chip said, "starting Monday."

"Knowing Ralston as *we* do," Aker said with a laugh, "I doubt it. Anyway, good luck."

That afternoon, Chip could hardly sit through his last class. When it ended, he hurried across the campus to Assembly Hall and up the back stairs to the coaches' offices. Henry Rockwell was working on some scouting notes when Chip knocked on his door, but he pushed them aside.

"Hello, Chip. Come in. You look as if you've got something important on your mind."

"I have. Whittemore and Aker and Jacobs."

"Oh, that again. Let's hear it."

Chip told Rockwell about the progress he had made, about Whittemore's apology, the reaction of Aker and Jacobs, and the feeling of the members of the team. When he finished, Rockwell smiled his crooked smile and nodded in approval. "You *have* been busy. Now what?"

"That's what I wanted to ask you. I had planned to talk to the dean—"

Rockwell shook his head vigorously. "Oh, no, Chip. That would only stir the whole thing up again."

"What should I do, Coach?"

"Go see Coach Ralston. And there's no time like the present. He's in his office right now."

Chip took a deep breath. "All right," he said. "Here goes!"

He found Ralston sitting with his back to his desk and staring moodily out the window. The coach was so absorbed in his thoughts that he didn't hear the knock on the door or Chip enter. The big coach whirled his chair around and started in surprise when he saw Chip.

"Oh, hello, Chip. How long have you been standing there?" He waved toward a chair. "Come in, sit down."

Curly Ralston studied Chip for a moment. "Now don't tell me you want to come out to practice?"

"That's right, Coach," Chip said smiling. "Doc Terring said I could come out Monday and do some running. In fact, he said I might he able to play a little against Western."

"With *that* shoulder? Uh-uh!"

"But Murph Kelly said he could put a shock cast on it. He said you could hit one of those with an ax, and it wouldn't hurt."

Ralston grunted. "That's probably true. How about throwing?"

"I guess I won't be able to throw anymore this year."

"Could you handle the ball?"

"Sure, Coach. Look at this!" Chip got to his feet and used his hands to fake imaginary handoffs.

Ralston nodded. "That would help. But don't get your hopes up. You're still on the nonplaying list until you get Doc Terring's OK. In writing!"

Chip was halfway to the door before he remembered the major purpose of his visit. He turned back toward the desk. "I wanted to talk to you about something else, Coach. About Whittemore, Aker, and Jacobs."

The frown lines between Coach Ralston's eyes deepened, and his strong jaw firmed. "What about them?" he asked sharply.

"Well, Coach, they've apologized to one another and they want another chance. We—well, the rest of the players and I—would like to help them."

"Help them?"

"Yes, sir. The team needs help, but we feel that *they* need help too."

Ralston turned his chair slowly around so that he faced the window again. After a long silence he spoke over his shoulder. "You're right about helping Whittemore and the touchdown twins. They can come back, but I want it clearly understood that they are *not* being given another chance just to help us win games. And I want all three of them in my office before the next practice. Is that clear?"

"Yes, sir," Chip said happily, turning away. "Yes, sir!"

Chip went into action as soon as he left Ralston's office. He hurried back to Grayson's, where he found Philip Whittemore behind the fountain.

"Good news, Whitty!" he cried. "Coach said to report to his office before practice Monday. How about that?"

"You're kidding!"

"Nope."

Whittemore's excited "Yes!" startled the customers at the fountain. Then he got serious. "How about Aker and Jacobs?"

"Same thing. I'm on my way to tell them now. Be back in a few minutes."

Aker and Jacobs were as surprised as Whittemore had been, but they were also a bit nervous. "I don't know how you did it," Jacobs said. "You mean we don't have to do any more apologizing?"

"Nope."

"But we do have to meet with Coach Ralston on Monday?"

"You got it!" Chip nodded. "Just tell him how you feel and that you *do* want to play football."

Aker sighed in relief. "I'll never understand it."

"Me either," Jacobs added. "Look, Hilton—"

"The name is Chip."

Jacobs grinned. "All right, Chip. I, well, we appreciate it."

"And you won't be sorry," Aker added.

Chip nodded and extended his hand. "I know that, Travis, Jack."

CHAPTER 20

Crossed Signals

THE CLOCK SHOWED four minutes left to play in the third quarter with Western leading 9-0. The Statesmen had the ball on their own thirty-yard line, third down, with five yards to go. Chip checked the Western defense and groaned. The visitors were using the same tight 5-3-3 defense they had used all through the game, secure in their knowledge that number-two quarterback Gary Young didn't have the arm to throw long passes. It was really an eight-man line designed to bottle up Fireball's line smashes and to cover Young's short passes.

"It's no good," Chip murmured, glancing along the bench. Whitty, Aker, and Jacobs were ready and waiting, watching Ralston with eager eyes. With Aker and Jacobs to throw from the right or left and Fireball from the deep position, Western would have been forced to change their alignment. And with Whitty to sprint deep into their defensive secondary, they would have been forced to back up, to worry about a long gainer against their defense. But just as it had been in practice all week, Ralston acted as if he didn't know they were on the field.

Ralston had used Chip twice in the first half, once to hand off the ball and direct the attack and once to kick out of a hole from the State University two-yard line. When Chip had handled the ball, Western had used a close 6-3-2 defense, virtually a nine-man line. His shoulder injury was known to every scout and team in the conference. Chip had counted on that; he had thought about it all week.

He glanced at the scoreboard and shook his head. His well-kept secret would be good for only one play. The way it stood right now, one touchdown would not be enough.

Fireball punted the ball down to the Western eighteen-yard line, the ball drilling through the air in a low, flat trajectory like a bullet. The visitors' safety man backed up, noting that the Statesmen covering the kick were far behind the ball. Right then the pigskin was nosing down, and he made the mistake of taking one last look at the blocking forming ahead of him.

The ball was just above his head when he looked up, and it hit him in the chest and slipped through his frantic grasp. The football bounded back toward the wave of oncoming Statesmen. He dashed forward helplessly as Biggie dove for the ball. A second later the referee blasted his whistle and pointed toward the Western goal.

Biggie Cohen had recovered the fumble!

It was State's ball! It was first and ten on Western's twenty-two-yard line, and after Fireball plunged for three yards through the line and Gary Young's pass into the flat was incomplete, Ralston bellowed for Chip.

"Hilton! Quick! Go in for Horton! Take Morris with you, for Anderson. Use a keeper play to get the ball into position and then kick the field goal! We need to get on the scoreboard quickly!"

Chip and Speed reported and then dropped into the huddle. "All right, guys!" Chip said. "I've got to get the ball in position for a kick! Keeper to the right on three!"

He carried for a yard, but the down placed the ball squarely between the hash marks on the Western eighteen-yard line. They hurried out of the huddle, and Speed knelt six yards behind center Mike Brennan and handled the snap beautifully. Speed caught and set the ball down in one smooth motion, just a split second before Chip booted it between the uprights. He could have kicked that one blindfolded! The score: Western 9, State 3.

The quarter had ended on the last play, so the teams changed goals. Substitutes Horton and Anderson came racing in to replace Chip and Speed, and they trotted off the field with the cheers of the State fans riding with them all the way. Chip breathed a deep sigh of relief as he dropped down on the bench. The stage was now set!

During the next ten minutes, Ralston sent Chip in twice to kick the Statesmen out of trouble, and his booming punts held Western even. On the last punt, Ralston left him in the game. Western played it smart and passed into Chip's zone—a long, high spiral that appeared to be going over his head and into the hands of their speeding left end. They didn't think Chip could interfere with his injury, but at the last second, Chip leaped high into the air and pulled the ball in with his *left* hand. He pivoted around, but the end was right behind him and dropped him on the twenty-five-yard line.

Western was still in their tight 6-3-2 defense, concentrating on stopping the running of Chip and Fireball. State was held for a scant five yards in three downs. It was fourth down on the State thirty-yard line. Chip's heart was pounding.

It was now or never! Western took their final time-out. Chip moved wearily over beside Red Schwartz. He knelt to tighten the laces of his kicking shoe. "Red!" he whispered. "Forget all about the blocking assignment on this play."

"Do what?" Red asked in astonishment.

"Be quiet and listen! Never mind what I say in the huddle. Just run! Run for the left corner of the end zone! Got it?"

The referee's whistle shrilled, and Chip turned abruptly away from Red to take his position in the huddle. He glanced at the scoreboard. There were just under two minutes to play.

The State fans groaned when the Statesmen formed in

kick formation. The Western fans began to chant the familiar "Block that kick! Block that kick!"

The ball spiraled back. Extending it at arm's length, Chip stepped forward, concentrating on the ball. Red and Biggie and Brennan and Montague were streaking up the field toward the Western safety man, and Chip's heart leaped when he saw the Western right end slant sharply toward him.

Then, just as the visitors' defensive line broke through the kicking pocket, Chip pivoted and cut out to the left, running for his life. The charging Westerners checked their rush and chased him as their right linebacker raced out to make the tackle.

Far up the field, Red cast a frantic glance over his shoulder and angled for the sideline. At the same time, the Western safety saw Red's move and Chip's run to the left. "Pass!" he yelled. "Pass!"

Chip waited no longer. He stabbed his left foot in the ground and made a left-handed pass, throwing the ball with all his might, with all the strength of his left arm.

It was a mighty heave, and he felt the sharp protest of the unused throwing muscles in his left arm just as the Western linebacker knocked him to the ground. The roar from the stands told him all he wanted to know, but he scrambled to his knees just in time to see Red cross the goal line.

Touchdown! It was a State University touchdown made on a left-handed throw by their injured quarterback! Pandemonium broke out in the stands. The Statesmen went mad on the field. It was a miracle!

Fireball and Soapy raced over and lifted Chip to his feet, practically carrying him up the field. Both were yelling something about fake punts and crossed signals and secret plays, but the roar of the crowd drowned out all the sense of their words and it didn't make any difference what they were saying anyway.

Chip's eyes shot up toward the scoreboard. All tied up at 9-9. And the try for the extra point was coming up.

But even then, even while he was thinking ahead to the kick for the extra point, his thoughts went back to his freshman year—to baseball—to the left-handed throw he had made from right field in the Southeastern game. He had been hit on the right arm by a pitched ball and couldn't use it. The Southeastern base runner had counted on his bad right arm then just as Western had today!

Biggie and Brennan and Montague were mobbing Red. Then Speed came hobbling in to hold the ball for the kick. They huddled and then formed on the line, and Chip's boot carried the ball high and true, between and far beyond the uprights, for a perfect kick! The score: State 10, Western 9.

Chip and Red trotted back up the field together, pounding one another in sheer exultation, oblivious to the thundering tribute of the fans. And the tumult of the crowd's cheering was still booming down around them as Chip and his teammates lined up for the kick. Chip glanced up at the clock. There was a minute and forty seconds left to play.

He put all his might into the thrust of his leg, and the ball soared high into the air and plunked deep into the Western end zone, out of play. It was Western's ball on their own twenty-yard line, first and ten.

The Western players were panic-stricken and hurried the play, and someone missed his assignment. Biggie Cohen and Mike Brennan crashed through the line with outstretched arms trying to snare the quarterback. In their powerful grabs, one of them knocked the football loose. Fumble!

Soapy was right behind Biggie and Mike and fell on the ball on the Western seventeen-yard line. State's ball!

Chip watched the clock and used every possible second in the huddle and on the play. He took the ball from Brennan three straight times and dropped down to cover it with his arms and legs and body right where he stood. Then the game clock read 00:00. Chip's teammates lifted him on their shoulders, and when he looked up at the scoreboard, it showed State 10, Western 9.

Sunday afternoon Curly Ralston and his assistant coaches worked feverishly in the head coach's office in Assembly Hall, discussing the strategy and the new attack he had devised expressly for the A & M game.

"We can call it the Convalescent Player Offense," Jim Sullivan said pointedly. "Everybody knows we've got enough players on the injury list."

"What about Whittemore and the touchdown twins?" Hank Rockwell asked. His question was directed toward no one in particular, but he was hoping Curly Ralston would make some comment. But the head coach ignored the thought completely and continued his study of the papers spread on the table.

A little later Ralston nodded in satisfaction. "Well, see you first thing in the morning."

Rockwell, Sullivan, and Nelson remained in the office after Ralston's departure and continued to discuss the new formation. Then the talk shifted to Whittemore and Aker and Jacobs.

"I think he should give them a chance," Rockwell said.

"I agree," Nelson said.

"Well," Sullivan drawled, "much as I dislike the touchdown twins, I'll have to go along with that. We know Whittemore would help and Aker and Jacobs just *might*—note that I said might—help. It's worth a try."

"Tell that to the coach," Nelson said, smiling.

"You tell him!" Sullivan retorted.

"Well," Rockwell said, pulling on his warm-up jacket, "I'm going home. We've got a tough week ahead."

The next afternoon, and on Tuesday and Wednesday, Ralston spent half an hour with Chip and Gary Young reviewing the new game formation and strategy. And every day on the field and on the campus, the tension mounted. This was the big game of the season and of the year, not only because it meant the conference championship, but because of the intense football rivalry that had gripped the two schools for over fifty years.

The game meant much to the regulars, but it was even more vital to the reserves; to play in one quarter of this traditional game met half the varsity-letter requirements.

Friday night every available hotel room in University was filled. And still the fans came, jamming the stores and streets and restaurants. It was a big business night for the local merchants, and Grayson's was no exception. Chip had hoped to see Skip play in the state championship game that night in State University's stadium, but Grayson's was mobbed. He and Soapy, Whitty, Fireball, and the rest of the staff had to settle for Gee-Gee Gray's radio account of the game.

Skip made a name for himself that night. It was his last high school game, and the fans really gave him a send-off. Skip deserved every bit of it. He played one of the greatest games of his career and won the game almost singlehandedly with his running, kicking, and passing.

After the game, the University High victory march started in the stadium and ended up in the business section of University, adding to the confusion and football hysteria that gripped the city. Skip stopped in at Grayson's just before ten o'clock, and George Grayson's employees took up where his high school friends and fans had left off. It all added up to a tension-packed preliminary for the big show scheduled for the next afternoon.

That night, Chip had trouble going to sleep. Tomorrow's game would be the biggest game of his life: the first college championship game he had played as captain of a team and one that would have a big bearing on his standing as an all-American player. He was planning ahead for the next day, thinking about the game and his arm and the touchdown twins and Ralston and A & M—for hours, it seemed, until at last he fell asleep.

CHAPTER 21

End-Zone Disaster

EVERY SEAT in University Stadium was filled! The massive array of color—State University's red, white, and blue, and the visitors' orange and yellow—created a brilliant display of excitement. It rivaled the tranquil natural beauty of the white clouds playing across the bright blue sky. Tailgaters arrived even earlier than usual to get their prime parking spaces and begin their cookouts on this game day.

Out on the field, Chip and Fireball took turns booting the ball to Gary Young, Travis Aker, and Jack Jacobs. Fireball drilled one of his low, cannonball-like spirals, and Chip watched as Aker yelled for the ball and pulled it in on a dead run.

That was the way Aker and Jacobs had put out all week. They had worked at top speed during every minute of the practices and shown tremendous snap and drive when running through the plays. Following the Western game, Chip had feared that they might lapse back into their shells, but the touchdown twins had given no indication that they resented sitting the bench.

A & M won the toss and elected to receive. Chip chose to defend the north goal so the Statesmen would have the wind at their backs. His kickoff carried into the end zone and out of bounds. A & M took over on their own twenty-yard line, first and ten.

State's forward line, battling as it had all season, held the visitors to four scant yards in three downs. After several punt exchanges, Chip managed to break away and sprint to the Aggies' thirty. Three plays later, with the ball resting on the A & M twenty-three-yard line, Speed limped in to hold the ball. Chip kicked a perfect placement for the first score of the game.

The State fans went wild as the band erupted in celebration. But it was the last time they had cause to rejoice during the first half. Thereafter, the Statesmen could do nothing right, and the Aggies could do nothing wrong. It might have been a different story if Speed and Ace had been in the game and in shape. As it was, Coach Ralston was forced to shuffle his makeshift backfield time and again, but to no avail.

Chip managed to break away a little later. Rockwell elbowed Ralston as he watched. "Look to the right," he said. "Look at Whittemore, Aker, and Jacobs."

The three prodigal sons were out on the edge of the field yelling for all they were worth, standing side by side with the rest of the reserves and cheering for Chip and their weary teammates. But to Henry Rockwell's disappointment, the head coach turned back to the field, apparently indifferent to the earnest trio's showing.

A & M's candidate for all-American honors, a clever halfback named Kerwin Bailey, was breaking the game wide open. Alternating as an end and a flanker, he bewildered Anderson and Horton—cutting past them, reversing, buttonhooking, and using his sharp cuts to snare passes in their zones. He tallied twice in the first quarter and again just before the end of the second period.

At the half A & M led 19-3.

Between halves, Murph Kelly studied Chip's face and tested the shock cast. "All right?" he asked.

Chip nodded. "Sure, Murph. Fine."

"You don't *look* fine."

Murph was dead right. He wasn't fine by a long shot. The Aggies had given him a rough time, tackling him viciously and dumping him hard every time he carried the ball. There was nothing dirty about their play, but they weren't giving him a chance to get on track, bad shoulder notwithstanding.

His muscles were fighting every command, aching and protesting and sluggishly obeying his will. He looked at his teammates. They were tired too. Like himself, Soapy, Biggie, Fireball, Red, Brennan, O'Malley, Maxim, and Montague had played practically every offensive series through nine straight games. They had never faltered and they had never quit. That was what football was all about, he reflected. A player gave all he had and then forced himself to give a little more. He fought for the team and his school and the coach and the game, loving the feeling that he was doing his best.

Coach Ralston moved from player to player, patting a shoulder here and there and saying a few words to each of them. But his manner and bearing made words unnecessary. Chip and every player in the locker room knew that every fiber of the hard-working coach's being was with them all the way. He could give it and he could take it. This was a man.

In the third quarter it started all over again. State received, and the ball came spinning end over end all the way back to the goal line where Chip waited. It was a good kick, and the confident Aggies came speeding toward him. The blocking was good up front; Soapy, Biggie, Red, Mike, Joe, and Pat each dumped a man. But the others couldn't handle the fast-moving ends and backs, and Chip went down under three of the eager tacklers on the twenty. In three straight attempts, State couldn't advance the ball, and Chip had to kick.

Now, for the first time, the Aggie attack stalled. But State couldn't take advantage of the opportunity. Chip tried

Fireball as a passer, but the A & M defense shifted just right every time, just as if they had called the play themselves. When Chip carried, he got clobbered. Only his superb kicking held A & M in check.

Early in the fourth quarter State had the ball on their own twenty-yard line, third and seven. Chip tried a reverse keeper and nearly got away with it. But Fireball's fake wasn't good enough, and the Aggie right back caught Chip on the State thirty-eight-yard line. He made a shoestring tackle and Chip went down hard. Too hard.

Ralston sent Benny Knight in to replace Chip and Junior Roberts for Finley. Then he walked over and sat down on the bench beside Chip. "Are you all right?" he asked.

"I'm fine, Coach. They just knocked the wind out of me. I'm all right now."

Ralston shook his head in relief. "I'm glad to hear that. Now, this game isn't over. We've pulled out of worse spots."

"We can do it, Coach," Chip said. He leaned forward and gestured toward the end of the bench. "Couldn't you give Whittemore and Aker and Jacobs a chance? They're ready, Coach."

Curly Ralston studied Chip's anxious face a moment. "All right, Hilton," he said. "You win!" He patted Finley on the shoulder. "All right, Finley?"

"Never better, Coach!"

Ralston nodded and turned toward the end of the bench where Whittemore, Aker, and Jacobs were sitting. "Whittemore!" he bellowed. "Aker! Jacobs! Here! Over here, on the double."

The three players nearly knocked one another over trying to be the first to reach Ralston. They pulled on their helmets and ringed Ralston, Chip, and Finley while the coach gave them their instructions. When the referee's whistle killed the ball on the next play, he sent all five in as a backfield unit.

It was third down, ten yards to go, with the ball on their own thirty-eight-yard line when Chip and his new backfield joined the linemen in the huddle. “We’ll pass,” he said, ignoring the relieved comments of the veterans. “Reverse 9 X! You’re throwing, Travis! On three, guys! Let’s go!”

It worked! Aker’s thirty-yard peg hit Whittemore on the opponent’s thirty-two-yard line. The big end made it to the Aggie twenty-five before he was pulled down from behind.

The momentum of the game had shifted now, and the State backfield became a symphony of action.

With Chip handling the ball, Fireball plunging into the line, and Aker and Jacobs alternating on tackle slants, the Statesmen scored in six plays. That made the score 19-9, and then Chip decided to go for the two-point conversion.

“We’ll run it!” he said decisively, grinning at the eager faces in the huddle. “Thirty-nine! That’s you, Jack! On three! Let’s go!”

He faked to Fireball and flipped the ball to Jacobs. The determined sophomore hit the line like a streak and bulled his way through for two points to make it 19-11.

A & M received, and Chip’s kick carried to the goal line. This time, the ball carrier made it only to the twelve-yard line before Philip Whittemore and Joe Maxim dumped him. The Aggies suddenly realized they were up against a new team, a team that was back in the ball game, alive, on fire, and determined to win.

They fought to move the ball for a first down and to eat up the clock, but the State defenders were fighting with renewed vigor and wouldn’t give an inch. The Aggie kicker punted to Chip on the midfield stripe, and Chip cut wide to the right. Just as he was about to be tackled, he lateraled to Aker. But the ball slipped through Aker’s hands! A & M recovered on their own forty-five-yard line.

Aker was upset and disgusted when he joined the defensive huddle. “My fault,” he said with remorse. “I was away and clear. It would have been a touchdown.”

"Forget it, Travis," Brennan rasped. "We'll get it back."

Chip looked at the clock. There were only four minutes to play.

The Aggies' drive ate up the clock as they moved to the State fifteen-yard line, where they were stopped. Then, on the third down, the quarterback attempted a risky pass. The A & M receiver bobbled the ball, giving little Eddie Anderson a chance to grab the interception in the end zone.

It was the Statesmen's ball on their own twenty, first and ten!

Chip called the play in the huddle; and when time was in, Aker hit Whittemore with a bullet pass just over the line of scrimmage. The big senior end threw off three tacklers before he was brought down on the forty-eight-yard line. Just forty seconds to play . . .

Chip faked to Fireball and went wide to the right on a keeper. Twisting and squirming, he made it to the A & M thirty-yard line. As soon as he was downed, he yelled for a time-out. "Time!" he cried. "Time!"

Ten seconds left to play! There was time for only one more play.

When time was in, he gave the ball to Jacobs on a fake dive play. Jacobs reversed and passed the ball to Whittemore just as the tall end crossed the Aggies' five-yard line. Whitty jumped far above the defensive opponent and pulled in the ball for the touchdown. The Statesmen were only two behind, with a 19-17 score.

Everyone in the stadium knew the play. State had to go for the two points. Two points to tie the score and to tie State and A & M for the conference championship.

A & M went into a close 5-3-3 defense as the Statesmen formed in the huddle. Chip called for a fake-pass play with Aker carrying over left tackle. "Make a hole Biggie and Whitty!"

"We'll make it!" Biggie said grimly.

"On one, guys!" Chip said. "Let's go!"

Chip faked to Fireball and handed off to Aker. Aker faked the pass to Whittemore and slanted for the hole Biggie and Whitty had made, a hole big enough to drive a car through. Then, a yard from the goal line, he fumbled!

The ball rolled across the goal line, and Aker dove frantically after it, his arms outstretched. Just as his hands reached the ball, the Aggie linebacker kicked it away and out of bounds.

Pandemonium reigned as the referee awarded a one-point safety to State University. The players, coaches, spectators, and even some of the officials had never heard of a one-point safety, and many of the State fans were still on the field and in the stadium arguing the point an hour after the referee had proven he was correct. It was right in the rule book, and he showed it to Ralston, Rockwell, and Chip. So the final score remained; A & M had won, 19-18.

There went the season and the conference title and all they had fought for through nine disaster-loaded games. All for the sake of one little point.

Chip and Ralston and Rockwell managed to edge through the hysterical crowd of Aggie fans and into the A & M locker room long enough to congratulate the visitors' coach and captains. Then they walked slowly along the aisle to the Statesmen's locker room. Pausing just inside the door, they surveyed the scene. Aker and Jacobs were surrounded by every State player in the room.

"But I lost the game!" Aker was saying. "I ruined the season for everyone, everything!"

"No way!" Biggie shouted, clamping his big arms around the touchdown twins. "*We* lost the game. The *team* lost the game!"

"Yeah!" Red shouted. "But wait until next year! We'll all be back!"

"Right!" Soapy yelled. "Come New Year's next year, we'll be eating strawberries in the Rose Bowl!"

CHAPTER 22

The Priceless Feeling

THE SPEAKERS' TABLE at the front of the hotel banquet hall extended clear across the room. Chip Hilton, seated at the head of one of the Statesmen's tables, turned to identify the people at the head table with the names listed on his program. Mr. E. Merton Blaine sat in the master of ceremony's chair, with Coach Ralston on his right and Coach Carpenter on his left. Seated in the keynote speaker's place was Peggy's father, Mr. H. L. Armstrong of the Mansfield Steel Company; he represented the Center for Sport, Character, and Culture.

A man with all the physical characteristics of an athlete sat beside Ralston. The program listed him as Stew Peterson, head coach of Brand University. Chip studied the famous coach. His tanned face indicated an outdoor life, and his broad, compact body spelled football. *So this is the famous coach who is going to guide Skip's future in football,* Chip thought.

Henry Rockwell, Nik Nelson, and Jim Sullivan were sitting together at the right end of the table, and several other men who Chip figured were University High School administrators and coaches were seated at the left. In between, he noted Bill Bell, sports editor of the *Herald;* Gee-Gee Gray, sports broadcaster; and Jim Locke from the *News.*

Athletes from both State University and University High School scanned the crowded tables to spot their parents and friends. Chip's eyes found his mother talking with Speed's, Soapy's, and Biggie's parents at a table in the center of the ballroom.

The members of the University High School team were seated at long tables on the right side of the speakers' table, and the State players were seated with Chip at several tables on the left. Skip sat directly opposite him at the head of the high school table. Chip caught his eye. Skip's face was glum, but it brightened briefly as he acknowledged Chip's smile. Then the smile disappeared, and Skip began to study his program.

After the invocation came the food. And it kept coming! Shrimp cocktail, soup and salad, an array of entrees from roast turkey and cranberry sauce to thick steaks, mashed potatoes with gravy, fresh vegetables, and then peach melba and ice cream.

Later, while the servers were clearing the tables, the State University Jazz Band played the University High School football march. The high school players proudly sang the lyrics, most of them in tune. Next they played the State University alma mater. Everyone stood up and listened to the beautiful words and music. Then everyone sat down, and E. Merton Blaine welcomed the guests as the program got underway.

Although he heard most of what the speakers had to say, Chip was thinking about Skip and Mr. Blaine. There wasn't any question about the purpose of Stew Peterson's presence. A major collegiate coach like Peterson didn't come clear across the country just to attend a local sports banquet.

When Coach Ralston was introduced, Chip gave him all of his attention. This was *his* coach. Chip was listening to him and wishing that all the athletes in the country could have coaches like Curly Ralston and Henry Rockwell. They were two of a kind: keen, alert students of the game; inspiring leaders; and understanding teachers with a strict moral code that brooked no equivocation.

Just as Chip had expected, Ralston gave the credit for the victories to the team and its fighting spirit. He had no alibis for the defeats. And being the great coach he was, he concluded that he was looking forward to next year! At the end of his speech, Ralston praised University High School's great team and paid special tribute to Skip Miller. When he finished, Chip was one of the first to stand and applaud State's great football leader.

Mr. Blaine then stood, waiting for the applause to end. But the people assembled there, and especially Chip and his teammates, weren't going to leave the slightest vestige of doubt in anyone's mind about just what they felt for their coach, Curly Ralston. Finally the applause died away and Mr. Blaine began to speak.

"I've listened to many speeches in my time," Blaine said, "but that was one of the greatest. And it was given by one of the finest gentlemen it has ever been my privilege to meet.

"At the beginning of this program I introduced Mr. H. L. Armstrong, who will now say a few words."

Chip watched with interest as the tall man rose to his feet, strode to the microphone, looked out over the audience, and began.

"It's a distinct pleasure to be with all of you this evening to celebrate all that is good and right about sports. I'm here on behalf of the Center for Sport, Character, and Culture, which seeks to promote sports as a means for developing and expressing all facets of human excellence, but especially moral character.

"In keeping with the spirit of this evening's celebration, the center is dedicated to fostering a sense of moral community within sports teams and empowering sports participants to experience the joy and pride of striving for excellence with integrity. All of which your entire sports seasons have celebrated.

"Over the next several years, it's our goal for you to hear more about ways that all of you—parents, coaches, and athletes—can become a part of this community-based program for youth sports. Working together, we can accomplish a great deal. Thank you for letting me be a part of this special evening."

Applause filled the room, and Chip noticed the smiles and nods of agreement as Mr. Armstrong took his seat and Mr. Blaine began again.

"Great words, Mr. Armstrong. Now we come to the first of the awards scheduled on the program. As you know, this joint sports banquet was sponsored by the University civic leaders in honor of the two great football teams gathered here tonight. We will get to them in a few minutes. First, Coach Stew Peterson of Brand University has a message of importance to every football fan in the country. Stew—"

Coach Peterson smiled and acknowledged the flurry of applause. Lifting a hand, he waited until there was absolute silence. "My part in this wonderful event is of extreme importance to my colleagues, who are members of the National Collegiate Football Coaches Association.

"Each year, as most of you are aware, the association makes certain awards. This year, it is my honor to be chairman of the awards committee. So I speak to you as an official representative of all of the college coaches in this country.

"Parents, coaches, athletes, and friends, it is my privilege to confer a trophy and announce—for the second consecutive year—the selection of the current year's all-American quarterback . . . Chip Hilton!"

The roar filling the banquet hall lifted Chip right out of his chair with the others. His teammates pushed him forward and lifted him on their shoulders in front of Stew

Peterson. They were yelling, and Peterson was pumping his hand.

Coach Peterson pressed the all-American trophy into his hands, and then his teammates put him down. Skip had him by the hand, and Aker and Jacobs had their arms around his shoulders; and the lump in his throat was as big as a football. He found himself alone in front of the microphone, and he couldn't say a word. He caught his mom's lovely smile, and suddenly he found the words to express his unrehearsed sentiment.

"To be an all-American player is truly a great honor. But it wasn't the biggest thing in football for our team this year. The biggest thing was to be a part of the team, to be one of those who stood side by side with the others and fought for one another in a common cause that was clean and good, where the greatest reward was the priceless feeling of knowing we had given our best for our friends."

It was five minutes before the audience quieted. Chip found himself back at the State University table clutching the coveted trophy in his hands, a thousand thoughts whirling through his mind: his mother, Soapy, Biggie, Speed, Red, Fireball, Whitty, Skip, Ralston, Rockwell, Aker, Jacobs, Peterson, Blaine . . . .

Coach Carpenter was presenting trophies to his players now, and Chip joined in the applause for them. Skip was the last to receive a trophy, and the ovation was deafening. Skip expressed his thanks and then thanked his coach. When it quieted, Coach Carpenter was so affected that he couldn't say a word; he stood there speechless, clasping Skip's hand.

Mr. Blaine came to Carpenter's rescue. "I have come to know Coach Bill Carpenter this past football season almost as well as I know my nephew, Skip Miller. Bill is a great leader and friend of youth, a man devoted to his chosen profession and to the youngsters he coaches. I know what he wanted to say to Skip and I am sure you know.

"Skip has captained and led two of Coach Carpenter's teams to state championships. At the same time, he has won great honors for himself. As you know, he has been selected as all-state quarterback for two straight years. And that brings me to an important announcement."

There was a dead silence. Chip and every person in the room knew what this was about.

"Skip has been imitating Chip Hilton for two years; his quarterbacking and kicking and running and passing—even his short-cropped hair!

"And I want Skip Miller to *keep* on imitating Chip Hilton. So much so that when Skip is a sophomore, ready to play varsity college football, he'll be ready to take Chip Hilton's place."

Blaine paused and turned to smile at Stew Peterson before he continued. "And when Brand University meets State in the Rose Bowl, Skip Miller will be calling the plays for his hometown team, for the school representing the state in which he was born."

A little buzz began in the back of the room, and it grew and grew until it burst into a deafening shout of surprise and jubilation. After Blaine lifted his glass of water in a toast, he cried:

"Here's to Chip Hilton and State's next all-American quarterback—Skip Miller!"

• • •

STATE UNIVERSITY, without an effective pivot man, opens the basketball season with three losses in a row. Determined to win the Holiday Invitational Tournament in the famed Madison Square Garden, Chip Hilton and his teammates overcome complicated situations by pitting ingenuity and teamwork against all obstacles.

Coach Clair Bee fans will find *Backcourt Ace* one of the most dramatic and action-packed sports stories in the Chip Hilton Sports series.

Afterword

MY MOTHER had a dilemma. She was finding it hard to interest her sports-minded nine-year-old son—me—in reading. Two years earlier, in order to encourage my reading, she had started me on the Happy Hollister fiction series. While the adventures of Pete, Pam, Ricky, and the rest of the Hollister clan were cute, I wasn't motivated to just pick up a book and read. I needed to graduate from the Happy Hollisters to more challenging and engrossing material. My mom was desperate.

Happening upon a book sale, she noticed some plain hard- cover books with sports titles—part of the Chip Hilton series. She bought three of them for me. To her relief, they became my favorite books, occupying a special place in my reading schedule for the next decade. Soon, I was a voracious reader, devouring every sports book I could find. She then fed this reading habit, scouring book sales, garage sales, and other locations for more Chip Hilton books. Little did we know that her diligence in finding the books would have such an impact on my life.

It was easy for me to identify with the Chip Hilton books. I lived in Valley Forge, Pennsylvania, and while I knew that VF stood for Valley Falls in the Chip Hilton books, I imagined that it stood for Valley Forge Junior High. It was a logical next step to imagine that I was Chip and that my good friend Jimmy Schuster was Soapy. It was easy to see how Chip's neighborhood pals could grow up playing sports in Chip's backyard because we were doing it too!

Oh, there were some differences. I was not blessed with Chip's speed, height, or weight, nor quite the athletic skill. I had a full family of a mom, dad, and three brothers. I lived in suburbia. But the values were shared. The books planted in me the philosophy that sports are one of the best tools for teaching values and in breaking down barriers between people. They reinforced the concepts of right and wrong, that truth triumphs in the end, that each person we encounter is important, and that the chemistry of a group is as important as individual skills.

Chip Hilton was my companion on rainy afternoons, before bedtimes, on long car trips, and on Saturday mornings. While I never met Clair Bee, the author, he was my personal coach, preparing me for my school athletic endeavors.

In 1980, while a student at Wake Forest University, my mother excitedly sent me an article from *Sports Illustrated* written by Jack McCallum about Clair Bee and Chip. As I eagerly read about the background of the series, I realized for the first time that I was not alone in my devotion to the books. Uncharacteristically, I picked up a piece of fraternity stationery and wrote a note to Jack, thanking him for the article and sharing my story with him.

After a few years of graduate school and transitions, I found myself in the sports television business. In the back of my head was the notion that Chip Hilton could be revived for a new audience—first with books and perhaps later through other media. After all, the Hardy Boys and Nancy Drew, contemporaries of Chip Hilton, were still around. There also was a void of quality sports fiction. I was sure it could work—but how could it get done?

Over the years I would work on the idea for a few months, make some progress, run into a roadblock, and put it back in the file. Finally, in 1994, a phone call elicited information that a friend of the Clair Bee family could put me in touch with them. Within one day I had the fax number. Within two days Cindy Farley, Coach Bee's daughter, and her husband, Randy, had read my first letter.

Space does not permit me to share all about my friendship with the Farleys. As their business representative, it has been my privilege to see Cindy and Randy fulfill their promise to Coach Bee by having the series republished in these paperbacks by Broadman & Holman. As their friend, I have seen them rejoice in the good news, endure the bad, and await God's timing for developments in their lives. As a parent, I have the greatest admiration of them as educators—teachers in an international school in Jakarta, Indonesia. As a Chip Hilton fan, I am pleased that they have maintained a careful stewardship of the series in order to impact the lives of youth.

I have now learned that there are thousands of us—the Hiltonites—people so devoted to the books that we have offered our assistance to help them become popular again. I have encountered coaches, sports executives, administrators, and media members whose involvement in sports can be directly traced to Chip. I have met with men like Jack McCallum (who revealed that he had kept every letter he received after writing the *Sports Illustrated* article—including mine), Barry Hauser and Steve Jarchow (who have two of the biggest collections of Chip Hilton books in the world), and others keenly interested in Chip. We share a passion to use our positions to be positive influences on young lives—because wouldn't Chip do that? Idealistic—maybe. Effective—you bet!

Over the years I have been involved with some of the biggest sports events in the world, consummated deals, and completed many large television programs and projects. Yet my biggest professional joy to date came the day I walked into Barnes and Noble and found the Chip Hilton books on the "Favorite Series" shelves—filed next to the Dear America series. Chip had come home, to his rightful place in the mainstream of literature, where his stories could be read by thousands more young minds. At that moment I pictured boys and girls being able to read the goodness and light of a Chip Hilton book, instead of a horror or occult fiction book they might have chosen.

Humbly, I went home, picked up the phone and called Mom to thank her again. As we spoke, my tears flowed because I finally understood that her role in God's plan had been more important than just finding books for me.

JOHN HUMPHREY
Executive Director
VisionQuest Communications Group

Your Score Card

I have read:	I expect to read:	
____	____	1. ***Touchdown Pass:*** The first story in the series introduces readers to William "Chip" Hilton and all his friends at Valley Falls High during an exciting football season.
____	____	2. ***Championship Ball:*** With a broken ankle and an unquenchable spirit, Chip wins the state basketball championship and an even greater victory over himself.
____	____	3. ***Strike Three!*** In the hour of his team's greatest need, Chip Hilton takes to the mound and puts the Big Reds in line for all-state honors.
____	____	4. ***Clutch Hitter!*** Chip's summer job at Mansfield Steel Company gives him a chance to play baseball on the famous Steelers team where he uses his head as well as his war club.
____	____	5. ***A Pass and a Prayer:*** Chip's last football season is a real challenge as conditions for the Big Reds deteriorate. Somehow he must keep them together for their coach.
____	____	6. ***Hoop Crazy:*** When three-point fever spreads to the Valley Falls basketball varsity, Chip Hilton has to do something, and fast!
____	____	7. ***Pitchers' Duel:*** Valley Falls participates in the state baseball tournament, and Chip Hilton pitches in a nineteen-inning struggle fans will long remember. The Big Reds' year-end banquet isn't to be missed!

I have read:	I expect to read:	
____	____	8. ***Dugout Jinx:*** Chip is graduated and has one more high school game before beginning a summer internship with a minor-league team during its battle for the league pennant.
____	____	9. ***Freshman Quarterback:*** Early autumn finds Chip Hilton and four of his Valley Falls friends at Camp Sundown, the temporary site of State University's freshman and varsity football teams. Join them in Jefferson Hall to share successes, disappointments, and pranks.
____	____	10. ***Backboard Fever:*** It's nonstop basketball excitement! Chip and Mary Hilton face a personal crisis. The Bollingers discover what it means to be a family, but not until tragedy strikes.
____	____	11. ***Fence Busters:*** Can the famous freshman baseball team live up to the sportswriter's nickname, or will it fold? Will big egos and an injury to Chip Hilton divide the team? Can a beanball straighten out an errant player?
____	____	12. ***Ten Seconds to Play!*** When Chip Hilton accepts a job as a counselor at Camp All-America, the last thing he expects to run into is a football problem. The appearance of a junior receiver at State University causes Coach Curly Ralston a surprise football problem too.
____	____	13. ***Fourth Down Showdown:*** Should Chip and his fellow sophomore stars be suspended from the State University football team? Is there a good reason for their violation? Learn how Chip comes to better understand the value of friendship.
____	____	14. ***Tournament Crisis:*** Chip Hilton and Jimmy Chung wage a fierce contest for a starting assignment on State University's varsity basketball team. Then adversity strikes, forcing Jimmy to leave State. Can Chip use his knowledge of Chinese culture and filial piety to help the Chung family, Jimmy, and the team?

I have read:	I expect to read:	
____	____	15. ***Hardcourt Upset:*** Mystery and hot basketball action team up to make *Hardcourt Upset* a must-read! Can Chip help solve the rash of convenience store burglaries that threatens the reputation of one of the Hilton A. C.? Play along with Chip and his teammates as they demonstrate valor on and off the court and help their Tech rivals earn an NCAA bid.
____	____	16. ***Pay-Off Pitch:*** Can Chip Hilton and his sophomore friends, now on the varsity baseball team, duplicate their success from the previous year as State's great freshman team, the "Fence Busters"? When cliques endanger the team's success, rumors surface about a player violating NCAA rules—could it be Chip? How will Coach Rockwell get to the bottom of this crisis? *Pay-Off Pitch* becomes a heroic story of baseball and courage that Chip Hilton fans will long remember.
____	____	17. ***No-Hitter:*** The State University baseball team's trip to South Korea and Japan on an NCAA goodwill sports tour is filled with excitement and adventure. East meets West as Chip Hilton and Tamio Saito, competing international athletes, form a friendship based on their desire to be outstanding pitchers. *No-Hitter* is loaded with baseball strategy and drama, and you will find Chip's adventures in colorful, fascinating Asia as riveting as he and his teammates did.
____	____	18. ***Triple-Threat Trouble:*** It's the beginning of football season, and there's already trouble at Camp Sundown! Despite injuries and antagonism, Chip takes time to help a confused high school player make one of the biggest decisions of his life.

More Great Releases From The Chip Hilton Sports Series

by Coach Clair Bee

The sports-loving boy, born out of the imagination of Clair Bee, is back! Clair Bee first began writing the Chip Hilton series in 1948. During the next twenty years, over two million copies of the series were sold. Written in the tradition of the *Hardy Boys* mysteries, each book in this 23-volume series is a positive-themed tale of human relationships, good sportsmanship, and positive influences—things especially crucial to young boys. Through these larger-than-life fictional characters, countless young people have been exposed to stories that helped shape their lives.

WELCOME BACK, CHIP HILTON!

Start collecting your complete Chip Hilton series today

Vol. 1 - Touchdown Pass
0-8054-1686-2

Vol. 2 - Championship Ball
0-8054-1815-6
Vol. 3 - Strike Three!
0-8054-1816-4
Vol. 4 - Clutch Hitter!
0-8054-1817-2
Vol. 5 - A Pass and a Prayer
0-8054-1987-X
Vol. 6 - Hoop Crazy
0-8054-1988-8
Vol. 7 - Pitchers' Duel
0-8054-1989-6
Vol. 8 - Dugout Jinx
0-8054-1990-X
Vol. 9 - Freshman Quarterback
0-8054-1991-8
Vol. 10 - Backboard Fever
0-8054-1992-6
Vol. 11 - Fence Busters
0-8054-1993-4
Vol. 12 - Ten Seconds to Play!
0-8054-1994-2
Vol. 13 - Fourth Down Showdown
0-8054-2092-4
Vol. 14 - Tournament Crisis
0-8054-2093-2
Vol. 15 - Hardcourt Upset
0-8054-2094-0
Vol. 16- Pay-Off Pitch
0-8054-2095-9
Vol. 17 - No-Hitter
0-8054-2096-7
Vol. 18- Triple-Threat Trouble
0-8054-2097-5

Available at fine bookstores everywhere.